FEAST OF FURY

All Skye Fargo wanted was a meal for himself and Imogene, the girl he had rescued from Cheyenne sexual slavery. But all the sweaty cook cooked up was a storm. "You be injun?" he asked the girl. "Injuns don't eat here."

Two drifters backed his play. "Get the squaw," the dough-faced one ordered. "Me an' Hardy will plug him if he wants to make sumpin' of it."

Fargo dived out through the cafe window. Glass showered around him, bullets whizzed over his head, as Imogene began to scream.

Fargo pulled out his Arkansas toothpick. And knife in hand, he did the last thing in the world that the gunmen expected. He dove back in. . . .

THE
TRAILSMAN
111

BLOOD
CANYON

by

Jon Sharpe

A SIGNET BOOK

SIGNET
Published by the Penguin Group
Penguin Books USA Inc., 375 Hudson Street,
New York, New York 10014, U.S.A.
Penguin Books Ltd, 27 Wrights Lane,
London W8 5TZ, England
Penguin Books Australia Ltd, Ringwood,
Victoria, Australia
Penguin Books Canada Ltd, 2801 John Street,
Markham, Ontario, Canada L3R 1B4
Penguin Books (N.Z.) Ltd, 182-190 Wairau Road,
Auckland 10, New Zealand

Penguin Books Ltd, Registered Offices:
Harmondsworth, Middlesex, England

First published by Signet, an imprint of New American Library,
a division of Penguin Books USA Inc.

First Printing, March, 1991
10 9 8 7 6 5 4 3 2 1

The first chapter of this book originally appeared in *Counterfeit Cargo*, the
one hundred-twelfth volume in this series.

 REGISTERED TRADEMARK—MARCA REGISTRADA

Printed in the United States of America

PUBLISHER'S NOTE
This is a work of fiction. Names, characters, places, and incidents either
are the product of the author's imagination or are used fictitiously, and any
resemblance to actual persons, living or dead, events, or locales is entirely
coincidental.

The Trailsman

Beginnings . . . they bend the tree and they mark the man. Skye Fargo was born when he was eighteen. Terror was his midwife, vengeance his first cry. Killing spawned Skye Fargo, ruthless, cold-blooded murder. Out of the acrid smoke of gunpowder still hanging in the air, he rose, cried out a promise never forgotten.

The Trailsman they began to call him all across the West: searcher, scout, hunter, the man who could see where others only looked, his skills for hire but not his soul, the man who lived each day to the fullest, yet trailed each tomorrow. Skye Fargo, the Trailsman, the seeker who could take the wildness of a land and the wanting of a woman and make them his own.

*Summer, 1860, in western Utah Territory,
beyond the Humboldt Sink,
where liars, deceivers, fast guns, and Paiute
met for a last showdown . . .*

1

Although he rode easy in the saddle, the big man astride the magnificent black-and-white pinto stallion trusted his sixth sense, which always warned him of impending danger: the Cheyenne were close. Too damn close. As he listened to the sounds of nature, his lake-blue eyes scanned the dense ground cover and the whispering pine for the slightest sign to betray their presence.

Moving the Ovaro north at a slow, cautious walk, he followed the eastern contour at the base of the Rocky Mountains. High above him, South Pass straddled the erratic Continental Divide. He knew the pass well, had been on it many times. He glanced through the canopy and squinted against bright sun rays ricocheting off the mountaintop.

South Pass stood in the middle of Shoshoni Chief Washakie's territory. But he knew there were no Shoshoni around at this time of year. Washakie had led them north on the Wind River Range. By now they were camped somewhere on the eastern banks of Jackson Lake.

The Cheyenne watched Washakie's movements. They always encroached on his territory the instant the Shoshoni struck their tepees and left their winter camp. Therefore, the big man knew he would find the Cheyenne encampment somewhere near the eastern slopes of the Rocky Mountains. He hoped he could get into their camp, do what he had to do, then work his way back out of it, all without being seen.

Suddenly the birds on his left stopped warbling. The Trailsman immediately reined to a halt. Easing his

Sharps from its saddle case, he scanned that area. He felt sure warriors were hiding in the outcrop of huge, jagged-edged rocks he saw.

A twig snapped on his right. So slight was the sound that only Skye Fargo's wild-creature hearing would have noticed and known it was unnatural. He shifted his gaze to his right and saw nothing but pine towering out the thick undergrowth.

Then all hell broke loose. War-whooping Cheyenne braves sprung from the ground cover and from behind trees. They descended on him with their knives and hatchets held high as other Cheyenne poured out the outcrop. Half-naked warriors were all around him, too many to kill. Digging his boot heels into the Ovaro's flanks, he shot and dropped two of the screaming savages who were in front of the horse, trying to grab the bridle.

The stallion snorted a protest, reared, and pawed the air. Hands grabbed the big man while others wrenched the deadly rifle from his grip. They pulled him to the ground and quickly relieved him of his big Colt. Other hands used his throwing rope to lash the big man's hands and powerful arms to his body. The free end of the rope was secured to his saddlehorn. A tall warrior leapt into the saddle and dug the heels of his moccasins into the Ovaro's flanks. The rope grew taut. Fists struck him as Fargo started trotting. A warrior stuck out a foot and tripped him. He stumbled and fell facedown, tried to get up. They shoved him back down and told the rider dragging him to go faster. The big man's muscular body swiveled on the rope as it dragged him over rocks and through weeds. Low-hanging branches and barbed thickets tore at him, ripped his clothing, and scratched his chiseled face.

He was barely conscious when the rider reined the Ovaro to a halt. Fargo's ears buzzed. His bloody mouth and nostrils were clogged with dirt and dust. His eyes fluttered open. Looking out the corners, he brought a pair of much-worn moccasins into focus. He'd seen these moccasins before. The buzzing in his hearing ceased. He took a deep breath, closed his mouth, and exhaled through his nose. The mighty gush cleared it instantly of bloody dirt. He rolled onto his back and looked up at the man wearing the moccasins.

The man squatted and in good English said, "Skye Fargo, I prayed to the spirits to bring you back to me. This time I will kill you."

Fargo believed the stocky medicine man would try. Kills Fast didn't take up the English translation of his traditional name on a mere whim. He had killed and scalped untold numbers of redmen—Shoshoni, Crow, and Sioux alike—long before hearing the English version.

The first white he killed was Lucinda Worthy, a girl of only sixteen. Kills Fast captured her during an attack on a wagon train on South Pass in the summer of '54. After her capture, Lucinda taught him to speak English. Then he cut her throat and added her red scalp to the long black ones that fluttered in the breeze atop his tepee poles.

Kills Fast now pressed the cutting edge of his scalping knife just below Fargo's hairline and growled, "Chief Many Horses isn't here to stop me from killing you this time. Pray to your God, Skye Fargo, while you feel me cut and peel off your scalp."

Fargo felt the razor-sharp edge break the skin high on his forehead.

The warriors encircling the two men nervously shifted weight to the other foot.

"I see the Trailsman's stallion," a deep voice boomed in the Cheyenne language. "Where is he?"

"Here," Fargo cried as the blade lifted.

The crowd of warriors parted. Chief Many Horses strode through the gap. He glanced at the red hairline fissure on Fargo's forehead, then looked at his medicine man and frowned.

Kills Fast explained, "These warriors caught him below the pass. Skye Fargo killed two of them." The medicine man aimed puckered lips at the two dead men surrounded by wailing women and children, then he continued. "The spirits say his penalty is death. I want his scalp."

"Wait a minute," Fargo yelled as he squirmed clear of the scalping knife. Rising onto his knees, he stared into the Cheyenne chief's dark eyes and went on, "They came at me with knives and tomahawks, not handshakes."

"He came to get my white slave woman," Kills Fast hurried to add.

They watched Chief Many Horses rub his heavily wrinkled face, obviously deep in thought, pondering how to handle the two adversaries. Finally he said, "First, we go into the sweat lodge when the moon is dark. I want to listen to what the spirits have to say. Untie the Trailsman and bring him to my tepee." Having uttered his wisdom, Many Horses turned and headed for his tepee.

Reluctantly, Kills Fast ordered two men to release Fargo. As the big man ambled away, the medicine man leveled a promise. "My blade will cut you many times, Skye Fargo. I will hang your scalp on the tip of a special tepee pole so my people will see it and remember it was their medicine man who took it from the big white man, the Trailsman."

Grim-jawed, Fargo said nothing. Two husky warriors, gripping scalping knives, with their bare arms folded across their hairless chests, blocked the big man's path. His eyes flicked from one to the other as he reached down the left Levi's pant leg and withdrew his Arkansas toothpick from its calf sheath.

Surprise washed over the warriors' faces. They glanced at each other, then at Kills Fast, as though asking him what they should do now that the white man was armed. Fargo boldly pushed the two aside and kept walking.

Behind him, Kills Fast's voice growled, "Sixty stone people, Skye Fargo, sixty. The ancient ones will weaken you with their hot breaths and take you to the brink of death. Then I will slay you."

Two other warriors darted ahead and escorted Fargo to the old chief's tepee. As one rapped on the tepee covering next to the door flap, Fargo sheathed the stiletto.

"Enter," Many Horses grunted.

Fargo pulled off his boots, bent, and stepped through the entrance. Chief Many Horses sat on buffalo robes placed in the west. Two middle-aged women, Many Horse's wives, One Feather and Pretty Grass, sat on robes in the north. One Feather broke and fed twigs to the small fire in the center of the tepee. Pretty Grass handed a gourd of water to her husband.

Neither female made eye contact with the chief's guest, although they knew him. They were being obedient to their teachings from infancy: in this case to never look into a man's eyes—any man's, that is, other than her mate's. They did this out of respect for the man.

The fear was that even the most innocent glance could be interpreted as a signal of sexual arousement, if not by the man, then by her mate, when the trio were together. Accordingly, Cheyenne women, like all other Indian women living on the Great Plains, never looked into the eyes of another man unless her mate told her it would be all right. Even then it was rarely done. Long-standing habits were hard to break.

Fargo knew enough Cheyenne to communicate with them. Sign language filled in the gaps. Fargo used both when saying, "Venerable Chief Many Horses honors me by asking me to sit in peace with him. It is unfortunate that two of your warriors had to die."

Many Horses replied, "What's done is done, Trailsman. They were hotheads, Kills Fast's men, not mine. Their allegiance is to the medicine man. He filled their brains with bad thoughts. When I'm away, he fans their fires of hatred for the white faces. You are lucky I returned when I did. Kills Fast hungers to claim your scalp."

"He nearly had it this time," Fargo muttered. His problem with the medicine man started before Lucinda Worthy had been taken captive. Fargo was much younger then, still learning his red relatives' ways and customs. He went out of his way to make friends with as many of them as possible. He found that in order to gain their respect and acceptance it was vital to respond in kind.

The red man's blood was the same color as his, their smiles and laughter were the same. They hoped, dreamed, and feared the same as white people. In many respects the red people were more organized, better off than their white counterparts. The Trailsman had found them to his liking.

He had honed his tracking skills on hunts with them. They had taught him how to use wild-creature hearing, a sixth sense common to his and their four-legged relatives, especially deer and antelope, the phantomlike elk and cougars.

Kills Fast, Fargo's senior by five years, had been a budding medicine man back then. He had a tendency to try his big white friend's patience, test his will, probe his mind, especially quizzing him about white females. Thinking the man was truly curious, nothing more than that, Fargo told him about some of the young ladies he had bedded in San Francisco and other places. Unwittingly, he had sown a seed in Kills Fast's mind, one that would come back to haunt Fargo.

After hearing about Lucinda's demise, Fargo had ridden into Cheyenne country, found Kills Fast, and confronted him with the tales going around about what he did to Lucinda.

Of course, the medicine man had admitted the stories were true. In fact, he had been proud of what he had done. He had gone further, explaining and justifying, "I didn't want to hurt her. The woman made me kill her. She started showing no respect for me. I caught her in Lame Bear's tepee and killed both of them."

Fargo had told him, "What did you expect her to do? Lucinda wasn't wise in the ways of Indians. You took her from her parents. Do whites steal your women? No!" Mad as hell, Fargo had warned him,

"If I ever again hear that you have taken a white female captive, I'll come looking for you."

They had fought an almost deadly fight with knives. Although badly wounded, Fargo's superior strength and a stronger will to survive had finally bested the medicine man. Fargo had pinned him to the ground, the tip of his stiletto poised to puncture Kills Fast's jugular vein. Fargo had taken the stiletto away. He had stood and said, "Next time, I'll send you to the spirits."

Kills Fast had answered, "No! The next time we meet, I'll have your scalp."

Chief Many Horses and all the warriors had watched the fight and heard what had been said.

Fargo felt directly responsible for what had happened to Lucinda Worthy. Now he wished he had gone ahead and ended Kills Fast's life. Gazing into the fire, he muttered, "He nearly had it this time." He blinked and the memory faded. Lifting his gaze onto the old man's wrinkled face, he asked in a stronger voice, "Is his latest captive well?"

Many Horses nodded, "She lives. But only barely. Kills Fast beats her." He glanced at his wives and they at him, then they lowered their gazes to their folded hands in their laps.

Fargo knew they had eye-talked. After a long moment of silence, Many Horses told them to look at Fargo when telling what was on their minds.

One Feather glanced up at Fargo and said in a quiet voice, "Trailsman, the white woman's misery is great. Steal her and go."

That's precisely what he intended to do. Nodding, he asked, "Where is she? Kills Fast's tepee?"

"Yes," Pretty Grass answered. "He keeps her tied up. When Kills Fast is away, he has one of his warriors watch her."

Fargo looked at Many Horses and asked, "Do you no longer have control over your people?"

Gazing into the flames, Many Horses grunted, "Not much. I'm old and weak, Trailsman, and my medicine man knows it. Soon I will die. He knows this, too.

15

He wants to be chief. In the meantime, he lets me live."

Pretty Grass and One Feather squirmed nervously and looked at each other. They're eye-talking again, Fargo thought. Finally, One Feather looked at her husband and suggested, "We will go into the sweat lodge with you tonight. Here is what we will do."

Fargo listened intently to the women's scheme for freeing the white woman and, at the same time, nullifying any attempt by the medicine man to prevent it from happening. He thought their plan had merit, would work, and said so. He asked only two questions: "Where will I find my rifle and Colt, and what about the horses?"

One Feather answered the first. "On Kill Fast's tepee floor just inside the door."

Pretty Grass answered the second. "Your horse will be saddled and waiting in the corral. Take any pony for her."

"Does that meet with your approval, Many Horses?" Fargo inquired.

A tired grin formed on the old man's lips as he nodded and said, "It is a wise man who councils with his women. They always know what to do. Now, we sleep, Trailsman. Preserve your strength, for you will need much this night."

Fargo watched the old man lie on his side facing the fire. One Feather covered him with a buffalo robe, then she and Pretty Grass reclined with their backs to the fire. Fargo added a handful of twigs to the embers, then he too lay down to sleep.

Somebody rapping on the tepee covering awakened him. He looked out the open doorway and saw it was dark. A warrior announced the medicine man had sent him to get Skye Fargo. "The stone people are ready," he said.

Many Horses sat up, rubbed his face, and grunted, "All right, we're coming."

Fargo noticed Pretty Grass's absence. One Feather put a finger to her lips, clearly cautioning him not to speak. Her eyes followed the warrior's soft footsteps as he went around the tepee and left. Then she signed, "Pretty Grass has left to make your horse ready. She will join us at the sweat lodge."

Outside, Fargo pulled on his boots and posed two more questions. "Where is Kills Fast's tepee, and the horses?"

One Feather shot puckered lips at a black-bottomed tepee on the far side of the open space where Kills Fast had threatened him with a scalping knife.

Chief Many Horses told him the ponies and his horse were hitched to long ropes tied to trees on the north side of the encampment.

Pretty Grass met them on their way to the sweat site, located a short distance from the encampment, near a pond. Fargo and Many Horses walked side by side while the wives followed in their footprints at a discreet distance. Nobody spoke.

Kills Fast sat on the trunk of a fallen pine. The doorman and fire-keeper stood near the bonfire, staring into the flames. Upon seeing Fargo, the medicine man stood and snapped his fingers. The lean fire-keeper instantly began pulling sections of blazing pine logs from around the fire to expose the sixty ancient ones stacked in pyramid form. The column of stones were white-hot, transparent. Fargo knew that the cruel medicine man intended to kill him and the others with steam. In so doing, the man would kill two birds with one stone: Fargo, his enemy, and Many Horses, his chief.

Fargo went behind the low dome-shaped lodge to undress and wait for the women to crawl inside and move to sit in the north.

The medicine man entered after them and sat on the immediate north edge of the low-built doorway. Fargo knew to sit in the honor seat in the west, so he preceded Many Horses, who would sit opposite Kills Fast. All were completely nude. They looked at the shallow stone pit and watched the first seven glowing red-and-white stones come in and be ceremoniously touched by the long stem of Kills Fast's pipe, then arranged in the pit. Silence was demanded while the initial seven stones were put in place. Their silence was a show of respect. The ancient ones would die after cooling and never be used again.

While the fire-keeper and doorman shuttled back and forth, bringing in the rest of the stones, Kills Fast used the time to taunt Fargo. "'So, my former friend, it comes down to this. Don't die in here, Skye Fargo. Suffer, yes, but don't die." He looked at Many Horses and said, "Remember, you were the one who asked for this sweat. I'm not responsible for what happens to you. The spirits will be." He glanced back at Fargo and continued, "If he dies, you will be directly responsible, Skye Fargo. We didn't invite you into our encampment."

"No, you dragged me into it," Fargo muttered.

"I know why you came. Dragging or riding makes no difference."

The sweaty face of the fire-keeper appeared in the doorway. He nodded that the rest of the stones were in the pit. Kills Fast told him to lower the door flap.

The dramatic rise in temperature was instantaneous. The bright-red mound of stones, none smaller than a large cantaloupe, cast a glow that lit the interior. Fargo and the women followed Many Horses' example as he bent and touched his nose to the moist ground, seeking cooler air to breathe in advance of what was to come.

One-half of a geode large as a buffalo skull had been put on the ground between the stone pit and doorway. It was filled with water and had a buffalo horn in the bottom of it. Kills Fast smiled as he poured water onto the searing stones. The ancient ones crackled, hissed, and spat. The resulting blast of steam was murderously hot on Fargo's back. The two women groaned. Kills Fast dipped and poured four more hornfuls in rapid succession. Fargo buried his nose in the hot, muddy ground, then willed himself not to move a muscle and took shallow breaths. Kills Fast burst out laughing and added even more water to the stones.

Pretty Grass fell onto the medicine man and clutched his arms, effectively pinning him. "Now," she cried.

Chief Many Horses dumped the entire geode of water onto the stones. A mammoth cloud of dense steam erupted. Moving swiftly through it, Fargo went one way, One Feather the other. She helped Pretty Grass hold down Kills Fast while Fargo stumbled over Many Horses' prostrate body en route to the door.

As Fargo pushed it open, a mighty gush of pent-up steam exploded out of the opening. He crawled out, closed the flap, and said to the startled warriors, "The spirits are angry. They told me to leave and for you to keep the others inside."

The doorman stepped on the bottom part of the door flap and gestured for the fire-keeper to help him. Fargo dressed as he ran back to the tepees. Knowing a guard was inside Kills Fast's tepee, he decided to flush him out. Smoke rose out of the upper vent. Fargo quickly moved the poles holding apart the vent flaps and closed them tightly. Then he dashed to and stood beside the door flap. The warrior and woman started coughing. The flap was pushed open. The warrior emerged rubbing his eyes and gagging.

Fargo's right fist slammed into the man's abdomen. A hard uppercut to the jaw and the warrior went down. He didn't get up. Fargo reached in and got his guns. The woman was tied to a tepee pole. Cutting her free, he asked, "Are you Imogene Talbot?"

"Yes," she gasped.

2

Twenty-nine days and twelve hundred miles later, St. Louis loomed in the distance. During all that time, most of it spent in raw, open country, Fargo hadn't touched the shapely twenty-year-old brunette, although all she talked about was sex—and without any shame whatsoever. Imogene would shed her Cheyenne-made tan buckskin dress right in front of Fargo, as though he were blind and had no feelings. She told him she enjoyed being naked, that it made her feel clean, close to God. Were not Adam and Eve bare-skinned in the Garden of Eden? At the ponds and streams where they camped, they bathed together but never touched except to play, and then only fleetingly. Seeing her nude aroused him at first, but he soon got used to it.

The young woman even rode in the raw. After basking under the hot sun for twenty-nine days, her skin was bronzed all over. Only the color of her hair betrayed Imogene Talbot as being a non-Indian.

She was a product of a union between Brother Noah Talbot—a towering man with unruly silver hair and a bulbous-tipped nose—and his gaunt wife, Sister Beatrice, both hellfire-and-brimstone Baptists. Fargo hadn't liked being in their presence from the moment he had met the couple in Kansas City.

They had turned back immediately after the Cheyenne attack on South Pass. Distraught over the capture of their only child by red savages, they implored the Trailsman to go find and return their darling daughter to their loving arms. Remembering what had happened to Lucinda Worthy, he quickly accepted.

Sister Beatrice gave him their address in Chicago and said he was to bring Imogene there.

During the long journey back East, Fargo inquired about Imogene's trials and tribulations with the medicine man, but only after she broached the subject. Her willingness, if not eagerness, to discuss the matter sounded more like a silly girl's lark than a gut-wrenching ordeal. To hear Imogene tell it, she thoroughly enjoyed every minute of her captivity, with the emphasis on the many times Kills Fast shoved her onto her hands and knees and plowed her patch from behind. "He adored me," she had claimed with a toss of her head.

Fargo doubted Kills Fast adored anyone other than himself, least of all Imogene Talbot. Early on he'd concluded her talking so much about the romps meted out by the medicine man, coupled with running around naked, were good therapy for her. The young woman was in the process of cleansing her mind and body of all the filth the medicine man had heaped on her. She wanted to be purified again, at least in the eyes of her God. And so, Fargo tolerated both her nudity and her frivolous talk. He told himself that in time both abnormalities would pass.

They didn't. Now, twenty-nine sunrises later, she still rode buck-naked and chattered about the romps without letup. Fargo said, "Time to pull on that buckskin dress, Lady Godiva. Otherwise, I'll have to fight men off you. We'll be back in civilization momentarily."

Reluctantly, she fed the hem of her dress over her head and let it slip down over her body.

On the outskirts of St. Louis they came to a great many wagons, mostly Conestogas, loosely assembled for the two-thousand-mile trek west. Settlers scurried about making final preparations for the journey. It was a funtime for the youngsters, meeting those of their own ages, getting acquainted, forming friendships that would last until death. Wagon masters bellowed orders and settlers quickly obeyed. "You, Ebenezer Murch! Don't forget to smear lard on that axle before putting on the wheel." "This wagon's kingpin is split. Whoever owns it, get a replacement."

Excitement and bustling activity were hallmarks of wagon trains in the making. Venturing into the unknown was on everybody's mind. They were about to discover the truths and myths so many people had told them about.

Of course, it was old hat to the Trailsman and the buckskin-clad woman riding bareback alongside him. As they threaded their way through the wagons, settlers paused from their chores and stared at Imogene. Fargo knew they wondered if she was the big white man's Indian squaw and whether or not they were on their wagon train.

Fargo reined to a halt next to a sweaty, clean-shaven, older man getting a dipper of water from a keg secured to the left side of a Conestoga. The Trailsman waited for the man to drink, then allowed, "Biggest wagon train I've seen in a long time. Where are you folks headed?"

The man glanced at Imogene and asked, "She Indian? I thought the red savages had black hair."

"Not a savage, mister. Say something to the nice man, Lady Godiva."

"I'm from Chicago," Imogene replied.

The fellow winced as his eyes flared and stared at Imogene. He seemed dumbstruck as he mechanically poured the remaining water in the dipper over his head. Finally he blinked, looked at Fargo, and asked, "What were you inquiring about?"

"I asked where you folks were headed?"

"Which group? There's three, so far. One's going to Oregon, the others to California."

"Taking the California Trail?"

The man nodded.

"Then tell your wagon master the Cheyenne are camped below South Pass. He'll know the danger and will be on the lookout for it."

A seedy-looking, rawboned younger man wearing a derby walked up to them; the man extended his hand to Fargo and said, "Thanks for the information, stranger. I'll be sure to tell him what you said. By the way my name is Josiah. Josiah Dunlop. My companion here is Barney Ruttman."

Barney's grip was weak and clammy, the very kind that warned Fargo he was shaking hands with a sneaky man. "Who are you, mister?" Barney asked. "You take up with squaws?"

"I'm no squaw," Imogene corrected. "And I'm not his woman."

"Name's Skye Fargo," Fargo answered. He glanced back at Josiah and said, "Just so you will know, there's still eight hundred miles after you clear South Pass. Most of it is the prettiest country you will ever see. Torturous, but pretty nonetheless. Fill all your kegs and barrels with freshwater and conserve it. You'll damn sure wish you had when crossing that torture chamber." Fargo touched the brim of his hat and nudged the Ovaro into a walk.

A redheaded female, hurrying around the rear of the Conestoga, collided with the Ovaro, stumbled, and fell. Fargo instantly dismounted to help her stand. He discovered the woman's temper matched that head of fiery hair. She slapped him twice and scowled, "Why don't you watch where you're going?"

"My apologies, ma'am, but I—"

A muscular man of about twenty-five and having black hair and a handlebar mustache rushed behind the Conestoga and interrupted Fargo's apology by shouting, "Get your hands off Jessie!" The fellow, who Fargo assumed was Jessie's husband, proceeded to take a swing at him.

Fargo grabbed the onrushing fist in midair and yanked the angry man to him. The fellow was a blithering oaf to come at him like that. Nose to nose, Fargo said, "I made my apologies to the little lady." He shoved the irate man into the side of the Conestoga.

Jessie screamed, "Leave Jeek alone! If you don't, I'll have him shoot you."

Fargo raised his eyebrows and muttered dryly, "'Oh, would you now?" He looked at the pistol stuck in Jeek's waistband and said, "Jeek, I'm going to mount up. I've got eyes in the back of my head, so don't try anything foolish. Once again, ma'am, my best apologies." Fargo turned and put his boot in the stirrup. He heard Jeek cock the pistol's hammer, paused, and said, "Don't make me leave her a widow. I will if you force me to. Just ease down that hammer before you blow your balls off . . . if you have any." Fargo continued to rise into his saddle and rode away.

Clearing the parked wagons, Imogene finally spoke. "You have balls bigger than all of Chicago. He could've killed you, shot you in the back. You're lucky, Fargo."

"No luck to it, Imogene. He wasn't her husband, not even her boyfriend. A husband or intended seeing his woman on the ground and a man standing over her would shoot first and ask questions later. Also, she wasn't wearing any rings. If anything, Jeek's her bodyguard. Nothing more. Bodyguards aren't emotionally attached like husbands and intendeds."

"I think I've seen her before."

"Oh? Where?"

"In Chicago. A long time ago. I could be mistaken, though."

"Makes no difference. We'll never see her again." He appraised Imogene's buckskin dress and suggested, "I'll fix you up with new clothes in town. New saddle, too. Your butt's probably raw by now."

"No, it's tough as leather," she said through a grin. "Want to feel it?"

"I'll take your word, but don't ask again." It was the first time she had encouraged him to touch her body. He wondered if Imogene had finally recovered to the point she needed a man, not behind her ass, but between her legs.

The main part of St. Louis fairly bustled with traffic and pedestrians alike. In the course of two blocks they saw numerous buggies driven by black men, carrying fancy dressed white ladies and gentlemen. Young boys carried wooden boxes half their size to delivery wagons. A fruit wagon piled high with watermelons rumbled past them. Teams of oxen pulled several

24

Conestogas toward those parked in the assembly area. Horses by the dozens stood hitched to rails and posts on both sides of the dusty street. Womenfolk crossed back and forth to shops, their maids laden with shopping boxes hurrying to follow. Gents, drummers, and wranglers wandered in or out of noisy saloons.

Fargo spied a two-story hotel on the corner and a barber shop that offered nickel baths on the corner across from it.

Imogene nodded toward a millinery shop that had women's clothing in the window, and suggested, "I know you're dearly dying for a drink of whiskey. Why don't you get one. I'll be in that dress shop, looking at clothes."

Angling for the nearest saloon, Fargo replied, "See you in a minute. Take your time."

He loose-reined the Ovaro to the rail out front and paused at the swinging door, to scan the crowd before entering. A brawl or gunfight might be in the making, and he didn't want to get involved in either. Shoes and boots lined the brass rail the full length of the long bar. Three bartenders poured drinks as fast as they could. A blue haze of cigar smoke hung over the men seated at poker tables. A wheel of fortune game spun, clacking past the larger-denomination bills. Several saloon girls wearing tight-fitting dresses that left little to the imagination plied both drinks and bodies to the poker players, especially those who were winning. Four men stood at the crap table placed at the rear wall. A fat pianist played a jaunty tune, his stubby fingers fairly flying across the keyboard. A leggy brunette holding a bottle of whiskey sat atop the piano, singing badly off-key.

Fargo pushed inside and went to the leggy brunette. "How about bringing that bottle of red-eye with you?" he said.

Without hesitation she hopped off her perch, curled an arm around his neck, and purred, "Name's Dulce Doll." She brushed his thigh with the bottle and added, "And I'm as sweet as my name, as tender as a baby doll."

"I bet you are. I wanted to ask you about that crap game. Is it honest?"

"Sure. Harold Keefer owns the saloon. Harold doesn't cotton to cheating. Doesn't have to. The odds and suckers favor him."

"Thanks, Dulce." He handed her a silver dollar, took the bottle, and swigged from it as he ambled over to the crap table.

Two young and lean cowpokes—Fargo assumed they were buddies on their first visit to the big city—stood at one end of the table, two well-dressed men in their thirties at the other. The cowpokes made nickel bets while the pair of citified men placed silver-dollar bets. One of the wranglers rolled, caught snake-eyes, and hollered, "Tarnation! Lost again!"

The stickman moved their nickels and the other men's silver dollars to rest in front of the man running the game. Moving the dice to Fargo, he glanced up at the big man. Fargo waved him off and dropped a two-bit piece on the come line. The stickman moved the dice to the man on his immediate left. Both citifieds made twenty-five-dollar bets. The fellow running things glanced at them, grinned, and said, "Twenty-five-dollar bets deserve a drink on the house." Over his shoulder, he shouted, "Helen, bring a bottle of our best bourbon."

Citified rolled a six for his point. After laying on odds, both citifieds—Fargo now believed they were drummers—placed an additional twenty-five dollars on the come bet area. The one handling the dice tossed an eight. Their place bets moved to the eight square. Both men replaced them with twenty-five more. On the next roll, he pitched a six, and they each collected fifty dollars, which they let ride. The place bets moved to the eight square. In short order the men's bets grew to four hundred dollars. It seemed the man couldn't roll anything but sixes and eights. Finally, both pulled in their money—and just in time, because the next roll came up seven.

Fargo looked at the young cowpokes and nodded toward the bar. He said, "Buy you boys a drink?"

"Might as well," one of them muttered. "That was my last nickel, anyhow."

They followed Fargo to the bar. After wedging in, one on either side of him, Fargo asked their names and where they were from. The one on his left answered, "Me and Homer, here, work on Mr. R. C. Vance's spread, the Rocking V near Wichita. Me, I'm called Red." When he doffed his hat, rusty-colored hair emerged. He raised his eyebrows and grinned.

"Mine's Skye Fargo."

"I've heard stories about you," Homer said, excitement in his voice. "Aren't you the one they call the Trailsman?" When Fargo nodded, Homer swelled up all proudlike, stuck out his hand, and half-shouted, "Gol-lee, glad to meetcha Mr. Fargo." Homer's grip was firm.

Fargo liked that. He said, "You boys want to be careful about whose dice you play with."

Both looked over their shoulders at the crap table. Furrowing his eyebrows, Red asked, "You saying that game ain't honest?"

The bartender appeared across from them in time to hear the remark. In a dead-serious tone of voice he said, "Better not let Keefer hear what you just said. Keefer runs the only honest game in town. Now, gents, what'll it be? I'm busy as hell."

Fargo shifted to bourbon, the youngsters stayed with whiskey. After the bartender had poured and moved down the bar, Fargo told them, "I'm not accusing, only suggesting that that pair of drummers have more than luck. And I don't know how the fellow overseeing the game or his stickman didn't notice."

Homer glanced over his shoulder at them again. "Are you saying those are crooked dice?"

"Like I said, I'm not accusing," Fargo repeated. "The house dice are honest. But you can't see but three sides of a cube. Nobody can without physically moving or picking them up." Having said it, Fargo put two silver dollars on the counter and told them, "Spend half of it on drinks. I think Dulce Doll will

27

satisfy the tug in your groins for the rest." He winked and left the saloon.

At the millinery shop, he found Imogene standing with two smiling female clerks and surrounded by boxes tied with ribbons and bows. Imogene announced, "Once I got started, I couldn't stop. I'd forgotten how much I get excited buying new clothes. Is it all right that I splurged?" She gestured at the boxes.

One of the clerks cooed, "She will look so nice in the dresses she picked out, won't she, Agnes?"

Agnes was quick to agree, "Oh, my, yes, Hortense. That buckskin dress isn't proper at all."

Fargo didn't argue. He paid up.

The two clerks almost buried him with the boxes. Hortense held the door open while Agnes clutched Fargo's money. Walking onto the porch, he heard Agnes say, "Hortense, put up the closed sign. We get to go home early today."

Fargo headed for the hotel on the corner. He had Imogene register for two adjoining rooms. The rooms were upstairs, overlooking the busy street. After dropping the boxes onto the bed, Fargo stepped to the window, parted the curtains, and pulled it open. Street noise spilled through the opening. He paused for a long time to look out. His gaze slowly moved from Keefer's Saloon to Ben Harper's Barber Shop. A tub of five-cent hot water sounded good.

When he turned to say he thought he'd have one, he saw Imogene had put on one of her new dresses. "It's a day dress," she said, and twirled for him to see.

While she looked nice in it, her braided hair didn't go, and he told her so. She quickly unbraided the hair and shook it to flow. Fargo sat in a chair to appraise the new Imogene Talbot. He asked, "What else did you get?"

Encouraged, Imogene stripped down to her red petticoat and began opening boxes. She modeled three additional dresses, two wide-brimmed hats, and shoes to match. Showing the last arrangement, she bent and kissed Fargo. Their eyes met during the encounter.

He saw in hers a craving, and in the kiss much encouragement. She bit gently on his lower lip, pulled back, and mewed, "Take me, Fargo. Take me now."

He opened the front of her dress, thumbed off the shoulder straps of the petticoat, and bared her breasts. Straddling his lap, she fed him her left nipple, which he rolled between his teeth before sucking in most of the supple mound.

Her head lolled as she moaned, "Oh, oh, that is what I missed with Kills Fast."

Fargo moved to the right breast and sucked his fill. "Jesus, that feels so good. Don't stop. You're wonderful. So good."

He raised the hems of her dress and petticoat and rubbed her buttock cheeks. She groaned, squirmed his hands to part the crack and move down to her hot curly patch. When he spread the swollen lips and touched her chasm, she gasped, "Put it in, Fargo, Please, put it in."

Fargo carried her to the bed and lay her among the many boxes. She had her clothes off quick as a Fargo wink. Breathing fast, excitedly, she rolled onto her stomach and pulled open his fly. As though seeing his length for the first time, she gulped, then gasped, "Oh, my God."

Before he could remove his gun belt, he felt her lips tighten around his pulsating, blood-swollen summit and draw down the foreskin. Her lips crept down the shaft until he felt them in his pubic hair. She came off it slowly, giving two inches, taking back one. As the crown slipped from her lips, they smacked and she whispered, "I've wanted to do that all my life. Taste a man. Feel him inside my mouth, on my tongue, in my throat. God, but you're delicious."

"Uh, huh," he muttered. "The best is yet to come." He stepped back a pace and undressed.

Imogene automatically got on hands and knees, spread her knees wide and her butt even wider. Entering the bed, he rolled her onto her back and parted her thighs. Then he buried his face in fluff and parted the moist, glistening lips and probed the hot opening with his tongue.

Imogene squealed for joy. "Don't stop! Oh, don't stop. I've never felt this good before. Deeper, Fargo, go deeper. That's it . . . Oh, my God!"

He moved up, swished his tongue around her navel, then addressed the begging breasts and tiny nipples again. Her hips raised and his crown mated with the slickened slit. She started wriggling and gasping, "Hurry, Fargo. Make . . . me . . . feel like a woman again."

His hands went under her knees and pulled her legs to his waist. During the movement the head slipped in and she moaned, "You're driving me crazy. It feels so good, so big. I want it all. Give it to me, please, oh, please."

Fargo thrust and went deeply. Her hips tensed, the knees raised slightly higher, and she began to tremble. He plunged through her several tight orgasms en route to flooding the deepest recesses of the velvety sheath. She moaned deliriously and joyously throughout the eruption.

When he softened, she clutched him and started crying. He reckoned she always sobbed afterward, but he was wrong. Her tears on his chest were caused by something else altogether. Imogene sobbed, "I wish I could die. I wish you had never come for me. I wish that beast of a man had killed me."

Fargo sat on his haunches. His brow furrowed when he asked, "What are you saying, Imogene? Death? You wanted to die? Good God, woman, you have everything to live for."

She grabbed his arms and pulled her face to his chest, wailing. "I'll never get a decent, proper man now. Not after him!"

"So that's it. That's what's been on your mind all along. You think—"

"Yes," she broke in. "Oh, I'm so ashamed. Nobody will have me now. Not even my parents and kinfolks. Everyone will stare at me and know that I slept with,

with . . . Oh God, forgive me! Please forgive me for my sins."

Fargo embraced and rocked her until she stopped crying. He understood her fears. White female captives of Indians were looked down on, viewed as vile, corrupt merchandise. It was dark outside. He could feel her eyelashes batting, tingling the hair on his chest. Fargo had been thinking, too, and now he said, "We will avoid the truth, you and I, about what happened back in Wyoming Territory."

Sniffing, Imogene's head left his chest, and she whispered, "Avoid the truth? How?"

"I will say I found you wandering aimlessly in the Rockies. You will say you fell off the pony and tumbled down a steep cliff while the Cheyenne were taking you to their encampment, before anything could happen. I'll back you up. It will be our words against theirs."

"That's a lie, Fargo. My parents would see through it, especially my mother. She would know different. I can't lie well enough to fool my mother."

"You can and will if your fears of exposure are strong enough. We'll come up with a plausible story during the ride to Chicago. You'll see. Now curl up on this bed and get some badly needed sleep. When you awaken, I'll be lying right here beside you."

Watching him leave the bed, she asked, "Where are you going? Don't leave me, Fargo. Not now. I'm afraid to be alone."

"Imogene, I need a bath," he said, pulling on his underwear. "I'm going to the barber shop across the street. Be back before you know it. If you're still up, get into one of those new dresses and I'll take you to dinner."

"I'd rather make love again," she said with a grin.

Fargo shot her a wink as he swung the gun belt around his waist. Going out the door, he chuckled. "That, too. Now that the cows are out of the barn, no sense in closing the gate."

The lid to a big box sailed over his shoulder and bounced off the wall across the hallway. He shut the door and went downstairs to her pony and his stallion. He stopped a portly, bearded man hurrying across the street headed for Keefer's Saloon and asked for directions to the livery.

Pointing up the street, the fellow told him, "Go two blocks and turn right. Can't miss it. Follow your nose. Say, do you know if those two men shooting dice in Keefer's are still on a winning streak?"

Fargo shook his head. The fellow hurried away. Fargo rode the Ovaro and trailed the Indian pony to the livery.

A boy no older than ten greeted him at the wide, tall entrance. "Howdy, mister," the lad said cheerily. "Stall or rung? Stalls are two-bits overnight. Rungs cost a dime. Hay goes with both. Oats are fifteen cents, and grooming two-bits. Nice-looking horse you're riding. That Injun pony's a mite scrawny, though. Wouldn't want to sell the stallion? Mr. Ormiston, he owns the place, would pay a handsome price to have him."

Dismounting, Fargo said, "Neither animal is for sale or trade." The lad watched him withdraw the Sharps from its saddle case. Fargo said, "Stalls. Give them good oats and all the water they want. How much did you say grooming was?"

The lad's face brightened. "Two-bits apiece. Do it myself."

"How much for dressing the tack and saddle?"

The kid walked around the pinto, looking at the prospective work, and muttered, "You came a long way, mister. It's trail-dirty. I reckon a dime for the tack ought to do it. Two-bits for the saddle. Fifteen cents for the stirrups."

Fargo looked at him and grinned. The youngster had jacked up the going price by fifteen cents. He handed the youngster two silver dollars and said, "Wash both till they fairly gleam."

Staring at the money, the kid chirped, "Yes, sir. I'll wash 'em down good." As Fargo turned to leave, the boy tugged on his sleeve and he turned back. The boy held out the silver dollars and said, "Mister, I'd take it kindly if you would put these silver dollars on the come line for me. Those guys at Keefer's are winning to beat hell. Mr. Ormiston made me stay behind while he went to spectate."

Scratching his neck, Fargo told him. "No, I'm not going to the saloon." He had every intention of going there, but only after his bath. Surely by then the man running the game would get around to killing them.

The kid's expression mirrored his dejection. He stuck the coins in his pocket. Fargo left him booting horse apples.

He entered Ben Harper's Barber Shop. The place was deserted. Aproned, Ben stood looking out a front window, watching men hurrying to the saloon. Fargo had to cough to get his attention.

Ben flinched, spun, and asked, "Shave or haircut? I pull teeth also."

"None of these things. I want a bath."

"Lye soap or fancy. The fancy smells like lilacs. Nickel extra."

He didn't want to climb in bed with Imogene smelling trail-dirty a second time, so he said, "Fancy," and handed Ben a dime.

The bath area out back was enclosed by a board fence. Fargo listened to the raucous saloon noise spilling over the fence while he undressed and Harper filled a wooden tub with hot water. No sooner had Fargo got settled in the steaming water than a youngster about the same size and age as the one at the livery rushed through the back door to the barber shop and came to him.

Removing his hat, the boy asked breathlessly, "Mister, your name Skye Fargo? Did you just stable a black-and-white pinto stallion over at Ormiston's Livery? Are you the one, huh, mister?"

"Yes, to all those questions. How do you know my name?"

"I took Robert's winnings from the crap game to him, Robert said you looked dirtier than your tack. Robert told me he reckoned you needed a bath, so I hurried over here."

"That explains how you found me. Now, why? And don't tell me you placed a bet for Robert."

"No. I get somebody else to do the betting. I'm from the telegraph office. The telegrapher has been holding a message for you for 'bout two weeks now. It's from a lady in Chicago. Thought you ought to know."

Fargo told the youngster to hand him his Levi's. Dropping a dime into the boy's waiting palm, Fargo said, "Thanks. It's from Mrs. Talbot."

"No it ain't. It's signed Abigail Tuggle."

3

Fargo had never heard of the woman, and it was too late to ask the errand boy for additional information; Robert's silver dollars were burning a hole in the youngster's pocket. The lad had raced to the back door and vanished inside the barber shop before Fargo could inquire. By now, Fargo thought, the coins would be on the come line. Telling himself he would check with the telegrapher later, he settled back down in the hot water and closed his eyes.

As he relaxed, his thoughts returned to the Abigail Tuggle message. He concluded the woman knew the Talbots. But why would she send a telegram? Had the Talbots moved from Chicago? Had they met untimely deaths? Those thoughts almost chilled the water. Desirable though Imogene may be, and willing, if not eager, to share her body with Fargo, he didn't want a long-term relationship with her. Twenty-nine days, plus the length of time it would take to get to Chicago from St. Louis, taxed his limit on the relationship, any relationship. Fargo had other things to do, places to go, and they didn't include traveling with a female, least of all Imogene Talbot.

His eyes snapped open the instant he heard gunfire at Keefer's Saloon. A wry grin formed on his lips as he listened to the shots, the saloon girl's screams, and tables and chairs crash on the floor. The winning streak was over. The patrons wanted out of the line of fire. It was none of Fargo's business. Let Keefer's people handle it. Fargo felt glad he wasn't standing at the crap table. He calmly began raising suds that gave off the aroma of lilacs.

The gunfire got louder. It had moved to the street. In front of the barber shop. A window pane shattered. Ben Harper hollered, "Help!" The back door banged open. The two citifieds dashed around Fargo's tub and vaulted the back fence. Fargo looked at the doorway and waited. Boots scraped on the floor within. A second later somebody inside poked a shotgun through the opening, then a gun hand gripping a pistol appeared on the other side.

Fargo said, "They went over the fence, fellows."

Two men cautiously stepped out. The one holding the pistol ran the crap game, and an aproned bartender the deadly shotgun. Both glanced around the area suspiciously. The bartender checked inside and all around the four tubs not in use. Satisfied, he nodded to the other man, who said, "Looks as though the lucky bastards got away. Search for 'em. Tear the town apart if need be. I want those cheating sons of bitches in the worst way. Get a rope. We'll give 'em hemp fever."

The bartender scaled the back fence and the man running the crap game hurried into the barber shop. Fargo finished bathing, dressed, and went inside the shop.

Ben Harper stood before a mirror, tending to a gash on his forehead. He glanced at Fargo's reflection and muttered, "One of them hit me with the barrel of his gun."

"You were lucky he didn't shoot you. Where's the telegraph office?"

"In the railroad station. Down that way three blocks." Ben pointed past the hotel. "Can't miss it. You'll hear the locomotives. Damn, this cut will leave a scar."

Fargo repeated, "You're lucky," then left.

A crowd had collected in the street in front of the saloon. Several men held coiled ropes; others rifles, shotguns, and six-guns. The gambler stood on the porch to shout their marching orders. Naked saloon girls hung out the upstairs windows to gawk and listen, their red-eyed customers trying to tug them back to the beds. The crowd split as Fargo ambled to the other side of the street and headed for the depot. Several of the armed men rushed past him, pausing only to glance in the spaces separating structures.

A train was just pulling away from the station as Fargo arrived. A cloud of black smoke gushed out of the engine's tall stack, white steam shot out the side vent. The engineer waved to Fargo and shouted, "You can make it! Betsy's slow in getting traction."

Fargo quickened his pace, lengthened his stride, and swung around the cowcatcher safely, just as the massive steel wheels grabbed and the locomotive lurched forward. He entered the depot and went to the telegraph office. He waited while the bespectacled telegrapher tapped out a message before stating his name. "Your boy says you are holding a message for me."

"Yes, Got it right here, somewhere." He leafed through a pile of messages, found it, and handed it to Fargo. "From Mrs. Abigail Tuggle in Chicago," the man added.

Fargo read: FEB 10 1860 STOP HOLD FOR PICK UP BY SKYE FARGO STOP SEE ME AT 712 MCCURDY ST CHICAGO ILLINOIS STOP MRS ABIGAIL TUGGLE. "That's all?" Fargo mumbled.

"Word for word," the clerk answered.

Fargo folded and stuck the message in his hip pocket, saying more to himself than the telegrapher, "Abigail sure knows how to pique a fellow's curiosity."

"I wouldn't know," the telegrapher muttered, and hurried to record an incoming message clicking on the key.

Fargo left the train station in time to see the train's caboose disappear in the night. He went to Keefer's Saloon. One bartender served drinks to the few customers still in the place. Even the pianist had joined the searchers.

The bartender explained as he poured Fargo a bourbon, "Harold put a price on the cheaters' heads. Two hundred dollars goes to the man who catches each of them."

"That two hundred for each?" Fargo asked.

The bartender nodded.

"He wants them pretty bad. For that amount, somebody will catch them."

Dulce Doll's reflection appeared in the mirror behind the bar. She sidled up to Fargo, eyeing him like a cougar on the prowl for something to eat. Her hand went to his left buttock cheek and rubbed. Dulce Doll's eyes widened and she pursed her lips provocatively.

Dulce Doll was a temptation, but he denied her. "Sorry, Dulce, but I just wandered in for a drink or two. Maybe next time I'm in town."

Rebuked, Dulce Doll moved to the next man on the brass rail.

Fargo rested the small of his back on the edge of the bartop and looked through the dissipating blue haze of smoke at the deserted crap table. To nobody in particular he asked, "What happened in here? Who exposed the cheaters?"

The bartender answered, "A young cowhand and his friend had dimes on the pass line. One of the slickers had the dice. He rolled for a point and the spots fell eight. He tossed again. The kid's hand shot out and grabbed them before they stopped rolling. Those dice were crooked, my friend. Then all hell broke loose. The rest is history."

"Anybody get hurt?" Fargo muttered.

"The kid," the man next to him answered.

"He's over at Doc Peabody's now," the bartender added, "getting the shoulder wound fixed up. Other than him, all shots missed flesh. Scared all the customers away. The saloon was in a real mess."

Fargo swilled his glass empty, put a four-bit piece on the bartop, then left the saloon. Crossing to the hotel, he heard men shooting in different parts of the city. Shots were fired at opposite ends of the street and near the train station. "They're chasing phantoms," Fargo muttered, "looking in all the wrong places, shooting at anything that moves or makes a sound."

He found Imogene buck-naked and sound asleep. He pulled off his boots and stepped to the window to look out. A full moon had risen. He viewed its diffused brilliance, then moved his gaze to the wagons parked in the assembly area. The canvas tops of the Conestogas, ships of the prairie, shone white. Soon, he knew, they would be covered with trail dust and dirt, clods of mud, not to mention sweat. Their ordeal on the baking plains, over the mountains and beyond, was just starting. He raised the studious gaze and stared west. Those two groups taking the California Trail, Fargo told himself, would have the worst of it. He could almost hear the Cheyenne drums on South Pass and envision the hellishly hot torture chamber that awaited all who made it past the Cheyenne. Releasing the curtain, Fargo undressed and eased into bed without awakening Imogene.

Her hand fondling his sleeping member and her lips nibbling his nipples awakened him. He glanced to the window and saw dawn's light, then looked at the top of her head and mused aloud, "Imogene, don't start something you can't finish."

She love-bit his left nipple and whispered, "Make morning love with me, Fargo."

"The best kind," he returned. He pulled her atop him and said, "Spread your knees and sit on it. I'll teach you how to bust a bareback horse."

She assumed the proper position and squatted. The penetration into the naturally lubricated sheath went deep. For the next ten minutes the ecstasy of Imogene's moans, groans, and whimpers joined those made by the bed. She rocked and gyrated while Fargo bucked and rolled his hips. After collapsing onto his chest twice, she entwined her fingers in his hair and hung on for dear life.

Afterward, they lay quiet for a while. Several roosters exchanged crows. A raucous jaybird lit on the windowsill, poked its head between the curtains, then vanished, squawking. Finally, Fargo said "I know you don't want to, but it's time we ride for Chicago."

He was about to ask if she knew Abigail Tuggle,

but she interrupted his train of thought when she replied, "I know. I went to sleep thinking about what you said last night. You were right, Fargo. I exaggerated my fears. I see that now. I have nothing to be ashamed of. I didn't capture him. He took me by force. But my folks don't need to know what really happened. What I'm saying is, I'll tell the barefaced lie."

"Good," he said. "We'll perfect our story on the trail. Whet and hone it to the point that it is unimpeachable." He patted her fanny to emphasize the last part. "Now, get on that shabby buckskin dress and we'll go get some breakfast. You can change into one of the new dresses when we see Chicago."

They dressed and went to a café up the street. Four disheveled customers occupied stools at the counter. Fargo didn't want to sit near them. He pulled a chair at the table next to the window and seated Imogene.

One of the men—by now Fargo reckoned all four to be drifters—looked over his shoulder at them and settled his nasty stare onto Imogene. The fellow's elbows nudged the two sitting on either side of him. They looked at him and he nodded toward the table.

The paunchy, sweating cook came from behind the counter to wait on Fargo and Imogene. In a tired tone of voice the cook asked Imogene, "You be Injun? Injuns and niggers don't get to eat in my establishment."

Fargo immediately pushed back from the table and stood to leave. Two of the drifters drew pistols and aimed at Fargo. "Get the bitch," the dough-faced one ordered. "Me an' Hardy will plug him if he wants to make sumpin' out of it."

Imogene yelled, "I'm not a bitch. Neither am I Indian. Get your filthy hands off me."

Fargo dived through the window. Tumbling on the porch, glass showered all around him, bullets tore through the shattered window and thudded harmlessly into the store fronts across the street.

Fargo withdrew his Arkansas toothpick and dived back through the window.

Like he figured, they didn't expect him to do that. As they swung to fire, Fargo's Colt barked twice. Blood spread on the two drifter's chests whom Dough-Face had ordered to grab Imogene.

Fargo rolled as Dough-Face and Hardy shot at him. Their slugs splintered the floor scant inches from Fargo's head.

He shot Hardy in the belly and sent its sister bullet drilling into his brain.

Dough-Face grinned as he pointed his six-gun between Fargo's eyes. Fargo was good as dead, and the drifter knew it. Dough-Face muttered, "Bye, bye," and pulled the trigger. And his weapon misfired.

Fargo was on him in an instant, slashing at his belly with the stiletto. Intestines and blood spilled from the wide cut. Dough-Face dropped his gun and started trying to grab the slippery guts to poke them back in. Fargo calmly reloaded the Colt while watching Dough-Face. He put a bullet in the man's head to end his agony.

Retrieving his Sharps, Fargo told the cook, "We didn't want to eat here, anyhow. This joint smells awful." He steered Imogene out the door.

They entered another café up the street. The two men and smiling cook inside were civil. Fargo's ham and eggs with grits, red-eye gravy and biscuits were good. Imogene picked at her meal. She did most of the talking, Fargo glancing up and nodding at all the right times.

Around a bite of buttered biscuit, she rambled, "I'll be glad to get out of St. Louis. Except for your teaching me how to do it new ways—I liked riding the bucking bronc best—there's been nothing but trouble in this town. I'm not complaining, mind you, not in the least. It was nice of you to buy me clothes. You didn't have to do that. Huh, Fargo?"

He nodded.

She went on after a sip of coffee. "Those people going west don't know what they're asking for. I know I wouldn't do it again. Not after knowing the danger. You know your way around the wilderness, the forests and mountains and all. How did you learn the trails to take? Weren't you scared? Did you ever get hurt? Huh, Fargo? How did you get by? Money, I mean. Nothin's free."

"I work," he grunted. "Only in a different way."

"Did my folks pay you to find me?"

"No. I was going that way, anyhow," he fibbed. Imogene didn't need to know everything.

"Well, they should have. Daddy has money. I'll talk to him about it."

Grim-jawed, Fargo replied, "No, you won't. Money doesn't mean anything to me. I get by."

Imogene put her fork down. Grinning, she cocked her head, leaned back in the chair, and looked into his lake-blue eyes. Finally she said, "You amaze me, Fargo. Really you do. You're rough and tough. At the same time you're the most kind and gentle man I've ever met. You're a study. You know that, Fargo? How many men have you killed? How many women have felt your muscled body pressing against them?"

He'd lost count. "Two?" he suggested around the last of the ham.

"Oh? What was her name? Was she as good as me?"

"I meant killings."

She shook her head. "I saw you kill four. You're not going to tell me, are you? About the women, I mean."

"Nope. You finished eating breakfast? You left most of it on your plate."

"Finished," she said.

Fargo paid the cook, then they left.

On the way to the livery she hugged an arm around his waist and promised, "Fargo, I'll make love with you every night between here and Chicago. I'll make you forget all those other women. You'll see."

He already had, but said, "The she-bear, too?"

Imogene poked his shoulder.

At the livery they found Robert cleaning stalls and an old man feeding horses. Robert looked up and greeted, "Howdy, mister. Get a good night's sleep?

Your horses and the other things are cleaned and ready. That's Mr. Ormiston over there."

Robert watched as Fargo walked around the Ovaro to inspect the kid's work. He'd done an excellent job dressing down the saddle and tack, too. "Nice work," Fargo said. He handed Robert two-bits.

Ormiston saw him do it and stepped next to the stall planks where Fargo stood. Shooting Robert a squinty glance, the old man told Fargo, 'He'll only spend it gambling." Robert took the admonishment in stride. Ormiston stuck his hand over the top board for Fargo to shake and went on. "Hoop Ormiston, here."

Fargo shook hands with him and asked, "How's Robert doing? Winning or losing?"

"Hell, he's winning," the old man snorted. "He's got a whole bag of money him an' that other kid, Dennis, won off craps."

Fargo looked at Robert anew. Robert cut a wry grin as he shrugged. "Who places the bets for your runner?" Fargo asked.

"Dulce Doll," he answered. "Dennis gives her the high sign and she meets him out back. Dulce gets to keep a third of our winnings for helping."

Fargo suspected she not only didn't place the bet, but produced the "winnings" out of her pocket. His stock of the generous whore shot up. He handed the kid two more silver dollars saying, "Have her place a bet for me, but don't tell her the money is mine." He shot Robert a wink and continued, "Next time I'm in St. Louis, I'll pick up my winnings."

"You coming back to St. Louis, huh, Fargo?" Imogene said.

"Don't plan to. Never can tell, though."

'I'll save it for you," Robert said. "You can count on it."

Ormiston snorted and went back to feeding horses.

Fargo saddled the Ovaro and backed him out of the stall to put on his saddlebags, bedroll, and other stuff.

Ten minutes later Robert stood in the entrance to watch them ride away. A gaggle of crows lit on the ground below a mulberry bush next to the livery. Robert picked up a rock and threw it at them. As Fargo and Imogene rode out of town, the cocks crowed.

During the ten days of easy riding it took for them to reach Chicago, they slept in hotels and inns, in haystacks, and on the ground. Imogene was true to her promise and made love with him every night.

When the skyline of Chicago appeared on the horizon, Fargo reined to a halt beside a pond and suggested she change clothes.

"Not before a swim." She had the buckskin dress off before she slid off the Indian pony.

Fargo set the horses to graze and joined her in the cool water. Afterward they made love on the grassy bank.

Fulfilled, Imogene sighed, then said, "I'll miss you, Fargo. Really, I will. And I don't mean just the love-making." She rolled atop him and started to cry.

He framed her pretty face in his hands, drew her lips to his, and kissed her openmouthed. She clutched his powerful arms and sobbed, "I don't know what I'll do after you leave. Oh, Fargo, I want to be free. I want it so much. I wish I could go with you, do what you do, and—"

Fargo touched a finger to her lips and said, "No, Imogene, you only think you do. Believe me when I say beyond the edge of your world is no place for a woman. For all its beauty, the wilderness is rugged, too much so for any female not born in it. Now, it's best I take you home."

"Will I ever see you again?" she sniffled.

"I don't know. Don't count on it. I rarely come east of the Mississippi." He kissed her, then rose and dressed. While watching her dress, he asked her, "Think you can ride that pony sidesaddle without one?"

"If Jesus came to town on an ass, I can. I'm ready to go if you are."

He lifted her up to ride with her legs down the left side of the pony. "Feel strange, perched up there that way?" he asked.

"I'd rather ride the bucking bronco."

An hour later they melded with the bustle of the city. Buggies and wagons of every description, legions of them, hurried past. Pedestrians placed their lives in jeopardy when dodging vehicles to cross the street. Nobody paid any attention to the big man astride the Ovaro, or to the young lady riding sideways on the Indian pony. In the first five minutes, Fargo had seen all he wanted. Relief came only when they entered a residential district. Even then the houses were too close together for Fargo's liking.

Imogene reined the pony to a halt in front of a gate in a white picket fence. "We're here," she said, and dismounted.

Fargo looked at the two big elms growing in the front yard, the blaze of color in the flower beds that lined the yard and front walk, and the white, two-story house trimmed in bright green. He saw Beatrice Talbot pull back a curtain in a lower-level window, then release it quickly. He heard her shout, "Noah, Noah! Hallelujah, Brother Noah, our prayers have been answered. Imogene's back."

As Fargo dismounted, the front screen flew open. The Talbots raced to their daughter as she ran to them. They met embracing, twirling dizzily. Finally, Imogene's parents dropped onto their knees and faced skyward. Crying unabashedly, they prayed, loudly giving thanks for the deliverance of their daughter while Imogene stood looking on.

Finally, she glanced over her shoulder at Fargo and screamed, "Please God, don't let him leave me," then ran into the house.

4

The Talbots came to their feet instantly. Sister Beatrice shot Fargo a pious, damnation glance that clearly conveyed, "You animal, what did you do to my daughter?" Then she fled after Imogene.

Fargo hitched the Indian pony to a picket while watching Brother Noah approach. Talbot came through the gateway, grabbed Fargo in a tight bear hug, and shouted, "Hallelujah, hallelujah! God has returned our little lost lamb to the fold." Shifting to a whisper, he said, "Pray with me, Mr. Fargo. Let's give thanks to the Lord for returning sweet Imogene to our loving arms." He let go of Fargo and sank to his knees.

The big man watched Talbot's hands clasp in prayer, tilt his head to face heavenward, and pinch his eyes shut. Talbot opened his mouth to speak to God, paused, and opened his eyes. "Well," Talbot began, "are you going to pray with me or not? On your knees, man."

Fargo felt like telling him that Imogene wasn't the pure, sweet thing he thought. Neither did God pluck his daughter out of that Cheyenne medicine man's tepee, although he probably helped. Fargo was the one who felt the scalping knife on his forehead, not God. He mumbled, "I'll remove my hat and stand here and remain silent while you do it."

Wild-eyed, Talbot yelled, "Repent! Repent!" Spittle came from the corners of his mouth. The man's face turned beet-red. Purple veins in his neck drew tight as a banjo string.

Fargo replied dryly, "Simmer down, Brother Noah. Calm down before you bust a blood vessel."

"Repent," Talbot continued.

"What for? I haven't done anything to make me think I need to. Get off your knees. You can pray later. Right now let's talk. I've got something to ask you, and I'm in a hurry." Fargo wanted away from the man and this picket fence.

Talbot rose slowly and spewed venomously. "Talk? Talk? What about?" Suddenly he frowned, lowered his voice, and changed the tenor of the tone in it, as though God wouldn't hear and strike him dead with a bolt of lightning. "Did those savages ra, ra—"

Fargo shook his head, then repeated the story he and Imogene had come up with. At the end of it, he said, "I need directions to 712 McCurdy Street. Know where it is?"

Talbot's eyes flared. He gasped, "That's where Widow Abigail Tuggle lives. Widow Abigail is a member in good standing at the First Baptist Church downtown. What do you want to see her for?"

Fargo suppressed a groan. He didn't want or need another serving of hellfire and brimstone. "That's between me and her," Fargo grunted.

Feeling rebuked and denied the chance to engage in gossip, Talbot reluctantly gave the directions. Watching Fargo mount up, he tried again, "Have anything to do with her late husband? John Tuggle was a sinner if there ever was one."

Fargo shot him a sinful wink, reined the Ovaro right, and slowly walked away.

He hitched the stallion to an iron rung on the post just outside another white picket fence, this one at 712 McCurdy Street. A small mansion, the house surrounded by the fence was three stories tall, painted yellow, trimmed in brown, and had a walkaround porch, the roof of which was supported by brick columns painted white. A weather vane stood on the pinnacle of the roof. Fargo noticed the wind blew out of the west.

He went to the front door and used the brass knocker on it to announce his presence. A slim black woman wearing a dainty white apron opened the door and surveyed him from head to toe. Her gaze moved past the big man to the Ovaro and surveyed him, too, before she said in a tiny voice, "Missus Abigail's resting right now. You can come back later. In 'bout two hours." She started to close the door.

Fargo stuck his foot into the gap and said, "Woman, I've come a long way to see Mrs. Tuggle at her request. I'll wait inside, thank you." He pushed the door open and stepped around her.

Closing the door, she said, "'I'm Neenie. Wait here. I'll see if she's up."

Fargo watched Neenie go up a wide, brown carpeted flight of stairs. The foyer in which he stood attested to the owner's wealth. A plush Victorian settee stood against one wall, a circular mirror framed in gilded wood hung at eye level above it. An ornate grandfather clock stood against the wall opposite the settee. Framed paintings decorated the walls on either side of two closed doors leading to rooms. A crystal chandelier hung from the cathedral ceiling. The clock began tolling the hour. Fargo heard it strike eleven times.

On the ninth tolling, Neenie came down the staircase and opened the door to the left of Fargo. Stepping inside for him to enter, she said, "Missus Abigail will see you in the parlor. She'll be down in a minute."

Fargo stepped into the widow's richly furnished and appointed parlor.

Neenie asked, "Can I fix you a cup of tea?"

"A mug of coffee, please," Fargo answered.

After she left, Fargo scanned the room, hoping to spot something he could sit on that didn't look spindly and fragile. Six chairs and two couches adorned the room, but to him, all looked more decorative than functional. So he stood and glared at the large oil painting above the mantel of a fireplace. He knew the fireplace was decorative. It was too small to warm the room.

The painting portrayed a man Fargo guessed was no older than himself. A rose garden blended into the dark background. The man held a rose and didn't look happy at all. He was finely dressed and wore a white sheepskin apron that identified him as a Freemason. The painting dominated the room. The artist had done the man's eyes—by now Fargo had presumed they were John Tuggle's—in such a way that they seemed to never move off the viewer's, even though he or she moved about in the parlor. Fargo tried, but John's penetrating gaze never left him. It was sort of unnerving.

Fargo stood looking out of a window when Neenie came back with a silver tray laden with sugar cookies, a pitcher of iced tea, and a carafe of coffee. She set the tray on a low, long table placed within easy reach of two chairs and one of the couches. The table also didn't look strong enough to support that much weight. Neenie poured a cup of the brew and brought it to him; then curtsied and left.

Fargo eyeballed the painting while sipping the weakest coffee he'd ever tasted.

A huge woman, so obese that Fargo couldn't imagine how she could ever be comfortable, entered the parlor and sat on the couch. She flicked open a large Oriental fan and began waving it close to her heavily perspiring face. Well, Fargo thought, it *is* hot. Sweat glued strands of hair to her forehead. Rivulets of perspiration coursed through her cleavage. The thin cotton dress she wore showed where the sweat collected in several places.

Fargo thought the couch would break for sure, but it didn't. Without looking at him, she poured from the pitcher and asked in a wheezing tone of voice, as though speaking was a chore for her, "What did you want to see me about, young man? Neenie said that you were here at my request. She told me you came from afar."

Fargo moved to sit in one of the chairs facing her. He crossed his legs and put his hat in his lap before answering. "I'm Skye Fargo, ma'am."

"Oh, yes," she wheezed, and now looked at him. "I recall sending a telegram to the telegrapher at St. Louis about a month ago, asking him to deliver it to you upon arrival with the Talbot girl. You did find the poor girl?"

Fargo nodded. "Safe and sound."

"I saw Brother Noah and Sister Beatrice at my church and learned what happened," she explained.

From the emphasis placed on "my church," Fargo concluded Abigail Tuggle owned it. From all the elegant furnishings and other expensive trappings in the Tuggle home, he reckoned she could. Abigail paused to gulp down another glass of tea. "I'm not concerned about Miss Imogene, although I am pleased to hear you found and brought her home."

Fargo watched her cram the cookies in her mouth. Her jowls bulged as she munched them. He asked, "Then, ma'am, why did you send for me?"

Abigail waved a bejeweled hand his way and grunted through the mouthful of mush, "I'm coming to it, young man.'

He watched a third glass of tea disappear. Shifting her bulk, she continued, "Two and a half months ago, the bank burned and—"

Neenie's appearance interrupted Abigail before she could finish. Neenie announced, "Dinnertime, Missus Abigail."

Without hesitation, Abigail heaved her massive body from the couch and said, "Follow me, Mr. Fargo. We'll continue our discussion at the dinner table."

She led him across the foyer to the other door he'd seen. It opened into a small ballroom having a harp and a piano. Abigail waddled across the highly polished maple-wood floor to another door that emptied into the dining room.

Fargo stood looking at a mammoth table and counted an even dozen high-backed chairs surrounding it, five on either side, and one at each end. A large oil painting portraying a much younger Abigail Tuggle dominated this room. The same artist had obviously painted it, for Abigail's eyes faithfully tracked the person viewing the portrait. She also held a red rose from the same rose garden, a duplicate of the one shown in the painting of John.

The table was filled with delicious-smelling food: baked chicken, a whole ham, roast beef, and a vast array of vegetables and gravies. No wonder she's fat, Fargo thought as he sat in one of the chairs on the side. Abigail squirmed into the one at the head of the table, in front of the painting. Fargo had the benefit of seeing how she was and how she is. There was precious little comparison. If it weren't for her facial features, he believed he was looking at two entirely different women, one in her twenties, the other middle-aged, about forty-five. Twenty years made a hell of a difference, he thought.

Two young maids served them. The one attending to Abigail obviously knew what her employer wanted. The girl ladled her plate with some of everything on the table. When the one serving Fargo looked questioningly at him, he opted for the roast beef and trimmings. She promptly gave him large portions of each.

Fargo thought Abigail would say grace before eating. He was wrong. Abigail bent to the delightful task and started gobbling down the bountiful harvest of food. It was obscene, the way she wolfed down the food. She chewed with her mouth open, smacked her greasy, fat lips, moaned her ecstasy. Fargo ate very little of his.

Finally, Abigail gestured for the maid to take her empty plate away, leaned back, and belched loudly. "Fine meal," she wheezed. "Sissy, what's for dessert?" she asked her maid.

Sissy gave her the choice of three, "Nanner puddin', Missus Abigail, or strawberry shortcake, or pecan pie."

"I'll have the pecan pie *and* banana pudding," Abigail said. She glanced at Fargo.

"Strawberry shortcake," he told his server.

While they went to the kitchen to fetch the desserts, Fargo tried to pick back up on their conversation in the parlor. "You were saying a bank burned."

The fan brushed before her sweaty face several

.times. Finally Abigail wheezed, "Not now, Mr. Fargo. Wait until after dessert." She closed her eyes and belched again.

The desserts arrived on a silver tray. Fargo watched Sissy slice the pecan pie into four sections and start to put one on a plate for Abigail. Abigail tapped the fan on Sissy's hand holding the spatula and growled, "What do you think you're doing, girl? He said he didn't want any."

Sissy knew what the woman meant. Sissy transferred the entire pie to the clean plate and set it in front of Abigail. A large bowl of banana pudding was placed beside the pie. Fargo watched Abigail's mouth open wide. She used her fingers to cram a slice of the pie into the maw, then followed it with a heaping spoonful of the pudding. The sight of her gorging herself was such that he lost all interest in his strawberry shortcake. Fargo wanted out of this woman's house.

He stabbed a fork into one strawberry and said, "Ma'am, I have another appointment to keep. Would you go ahead and say what you wanted to see me about?"

She beckoned for Sissy to approach and told her, "Get the peacock feathers and fan me."

Fargo pushed back from the table and started to rise. Abigail grunted, "Set back down, young man. You want to hear what I have to say, and you know it."

He checked his rise, sat, and turned the chair to face her. Nodding, he replied, "Please continue."

While Sissy fanned her boss, Fargo listened to one of the most bizarre stories he'd ever heard. Abigail began, "Like I was saying, about two and half months ago the bank burned. It was our bank, Mr. Fargo. Mine and John's and our daughter Hilary's. Banking hours were over. The bank was closed for the day. John and Hilary remained in the bank after the staff left. They did that occasionally, so nobody—I, least of all—thought anything about it. They worked alone well into the night.

"Nobody knows how the fire started. The bank simply went up in flames and burned down completely. Oh, the brick front still stood, but everything else went up in smoke. By the time the fire brigade got there, it was too far gone to save."

Abigail paused to poke another helping of banana pudding into her mouth. Fargo crossed his legs and settled down to hear the rest of her story.

Abigail continued, "The first I knew about what happened was told by two policemen when they came to the house to inform John the bank was on fire. My first concern was for John and Hilary. Surely they had got out in time. When I inquired about them, the policemen just looked at each other and shrugged. They hadn't seen John or Hilary. Nobody had. They didn't come home that night, either. I was worried sick for their safety. Maybe they had managed to get to the hospital, I told these policemen.

"They said they would check at the hospital. John and Hilary weren't there. It looked like they hadn't escaped. The firemen had to wait until the bank was reduced to ashes and cooled enough for them to look for bodies. I was there first thing in the morning and watched them probe through the ashes."

Abigail paused again, this time to fuss at Sissy, "Come closer with that fan, Sissy. You know Missus Abigail's hot and sweaty. Pay attention to my needs, girl."

Sissy came a step closer. Abigail picked back up on the story. "Where was I? Yes, I was saying I went to the bank and watched the firemen poke around. Well, they finally found the charred remains of two bodies. They wouldn't let me look at the bodies, told me it was too gruesome a sight, that they would take the remains to the morgue and I should go home.

"A detective and two policemen paid me a visit at the house later in the day. They said that while the remains were completely unrecognizable, they did know from the bones that one was a female and the other male. The detective asked if either John or Hilary wore any jewelry. Rings or bracelets. Jewelry like that. I told them no, but that John carried a gold timepiece in his vest pocket. Then he asked how tall each was. I told him their heights; five foot, ten inches for John, and five six for Hilary. The detective made notes, then they left."

She refreshed herself with a glass of tea, then went on, "That night the detective returned alone. He told me a fireman had found a gold watch and showed it to me. Even though it was blackened and partly melted, I knew at once it was John's. My heart sank, Mr. Fargo, because I now knew my loved ones hadn't escaped the inferno. God had called them to His bosom.

"Their coffins were closed, of course. Two days later I buried the remains of my John and Hilary. Then, when I went through John's desk in the study to search for insurance policies on him, Hilary, and the bank, I found the letter." Abigail turned and shouted toward the kitchen, "Neenie! Get in here, Neenie."

Neenie hurried to her. Licking a smidgen of banana pudding from the tip of her nose, she said, "Yessum, Missus Abigail, I'm here."

"Go upstairs and get that envelope I showed you. It's on top of my bureau." Abigail rested her elbows on the tabletop, looked at her guest, and said, "I want you to read the letter, Mr. Fargo, so you can see for yourself what I suspect happened."

Fargo suspected something sinister would be contained in the letter. Just what, of course, he didn't know. He sipped coffee while awaiting to see. Neenie returned and handed the envelope to Abigail. She removed the letter, quick-scanned it, and passed it to Fargo. He read:

ARNOLD, SPITZ & ASSOCIATES, INCORPORATED
INVESTMENT CONSULTANTS
212 FREEMONT STREET
SAN FRANCISCO, CALIFORNIA
December 11, 1859

Dear Mr. Tuggle:
In reply to your letter of October 2, 1859, I am pleased to report banking opportunities do indeed

exist in San Francisco, as well as other cities in the
California coastal area and inland.

I encourage you to visit our vibrant city at the
earliest possible time. Of course, you would be wel-
come in my home while here. In fact, I insist you
stay with Marie and me.

Enclosed you will find a summary of banking
activities in the San Francisco area and everywhere,
and a word or two about Arnold, Spitz, and
Associates.

I await your reply.

Sincerely,
Horatio Arnold, President

Fargo lowered the letter and looked at Abigail. She
snorted, "They didn't die in the fire. That lily-livered
son of a bitch has left me."

Fargo could understand why. He asked, "What do
you want of me, ma'am?" and quickly answered his
own question, "Go find them?"

"Yes," she bellowed. "I'll pay you a thousand dollars to bring him back, not Hilary, bound and gagged.
That little bastard can't do this to me. I want him to
suffer like I have all these years. Oh, God, how I've
suffered."

Fargo suspected more than revenge for suffering was
involved. He inquired, "Did the authorities recover any
cash when they searched the debris?"

"Not one penny," she answered smugly, foretelling
her next indictment. "John and Hilary stole all of it.
Robbed my bank. Cleaned it out. I want it returned
forthwith, Mr. Fargo. Forthwith, I say."

"Your bank?" he asked wryly.

"Yes," she thundered, the wheeze suddenly gone.
"My bank! I gave the runt bastard the money to estab-
lish the bank. I want it back. Him too."

Fargo realized the woman's ego had been severely
wounded. He could sympathize with that. She was
quite obviously set financially for life. Money was the
least of her worries. Abigail Tuggle wanted her man
back. Her suffering had nothing to do with it. He said,
"If, and I emphasize if, I agree to go on this mission,

55

and find them, but not any of the bank's money, then do you still want your husband returned?"

"Yes," she boomed. "But not Hilary! Hilary is no longer my daughter. I don't care what happens to her. I know she despises me. Will you do it, young man? A simple yes or no will suffice."

Fargo stood and began pacing while he thought. If John and Hilary had moved fast, they could be on the eastern edge of California by now. Armed with the Arnold letter, however, Fargo could locate them easily enough. And since theft and murder—the two unidentifiable corpses clearly suggested murder—were involved, Fargo decided to go on the mission. Accordingly, he had no compunction whatsoever about taking Abigail's monetary offer. He said, "I accept the mission."

Abigail wheezed, "Good," and stuck the last spoonful of pudding in her mouth.

"I need to know some things about John and Hilary. For instance, their current sizes and weights, hair color, and speech. Things like those that will identify them to me. I'm quite sure John doesn't look anything like the portrait I saw of him while waiting for you in the parlor."

Abigail twisted and shouted toward the kitchen, "Neenie, get in here." Turning back to Fargo, she explained, "An artist did a painting of Hilary last year."

Neenie rushed into the dining room, wiping her lip. She said, "Yessum, Missus Abigail?"

"Go get that painting of my daughter off the wall in John's study. Bring it to me."

While Neenie left to obey, Abigail covered the salient facts concerning her husband. "You're correct, of course, about John no longer being the man he was in the painting. Today, he's balding, has a long beard—graying, of course, flecked with red and black hairs—and has added weight, especially in the stomach and behind. He also wears spectacles. John's a timid man. He's prone to stutter when exited or nervous. His voice is tenor. He sang tenor in the church choir. Is there anything else you should know about him?"

"His peculiarities, ma'am. By that I mean, mannerisms."

He watched her eyes roll back, obviously deep in thought. Finally she said, "One. John pees in his pants when scared." Sissy and Fargo's waitress snickered. Nonplussed, Abigail continued, "Like when I argue with him."

Neenie returned with the painting. Abigail instructed her to hold it so she and Fargo could view Hilary. She was a pretty woman, her face more square than heart-shaped—the squared jawline caused it. Her eyes were deep-green, her tresses red. She wore a bright-yellow taffeta dress with large brown buttons down the front. A slim, fine-figured young woman—Fargo guessed she might be in her mid-twenties—she was obviously hell-on-wheels. Hilary had the look he'd seen so many times. He wondered if the artist had gotten her to pose in the nude for him.

"Hilary has a nasty temper," Abigail volunteered. "And the vocabulary to go with it," she added hastily. "She's twenty-five. Five hundred now, and five hundred when I have that little sniveling rat in my hands."

Fargo knew she referred to her husband. He nodded. Abigail sent Neenie to fetch her purse. When Neenie returned with it, Abigail removed a wad of folded bills and counted off five hundred dollars. Tossing the money onto the table in front of Fargo, she said, "Count it, young man, to make sure I didn't short you."

Fargo looked at the bills and said, "I trust your count, ma'am."

She nodded, sighed, and suggested, "Now, I need to go upstairs and rest. Bring the peacock feathers, Sissy. You can fan me to sleep. If you will excuse me, Mr. Fargo . . . ?"

Nodding, he replied, "I'll eat a helping of strawberries and shortcake, then let myself out. Rest well, madam. You won't see me again till I get back with your husband."

He watched as she heaved her bulk from the chair and waddled away, wheezing. His waitress brought him a fresh helping of dessert and watched while he ate. Fargo asked her, "Did they argue and fight?"

She hesitated before answering, "Uh, huh, all the time. Missus Abigail, she give Mr. John pure hell. Uh, huh, she sure did."

His dessert dish lay empty. Fargo set the fork on the dish, rose, and left. Getting into the saddle, he looked at the house. "Too easy," he mumbled. "I'll find out just how easy when I get to San Francisco, won't I, boy?" he muttered to the pinto.

The Ovaro knickered.

5

The big man astride the Ovaro rode into St. Louis at sunset ten days after visiting Abigail Tuggle. The letter from Horatio Arnold was folded and tucked in his hip pocket. During the ride from Chicago, he'd reasoned that John and Hilary had joined a wagon train taking the California Trail. St. Louis was the jumping-off point. The odds were against it, he knew—nearly three months was a long time—but the possibility of them still being in St. Louis existed. He went straight to the assembly area to check.

Ten wagons, mostly Conestogas, stood end-to-end, spaced apart to permit the teams of oxen that would pull them to be easily harnessed. The oxen grazed inside a roped corral a short distance from the wagons. Everything was ready for an early-morning departure the next day.

Fargo found the wagon master busy making sure. Setting easy in his saddle, Fargo asked him, "Do you by any chance have a John or Hilary Tuggle on this wagon train?"

"Not that I know of. You can look for them if you like, though. Names mean nothing. What do they look like?"

Fargo described them. The fellow shook his head, saying, "Don't think I know them. Where they going?"

"San Francisco," Fargo answered.

"I'm taking these folks to Seattle. They wouldn't be on my train." He turned back to his inspection.

Fargo rode down the line, anyhow, to make sure. He didn't see anybody who fit Abigail's descriptions.

Looking at the setting sun, he decided to wait in town until it appeared again.

At Ormiston's Livery, a grinning Robert greeted him. "You're lucky as a two-dicked dog, Mr. Fargo."

"Oh? What do you mean by that?" Fargo dismounted and led the stallion into a clean stall.

Robert explained, "You won. Dulce kept a dollar and eighty cents for her part. I'll go get the rest out of my bag." Robert trotted away.

Fargo unsaddled and removed his other gear while Robert was gone. The youngster returned and held out to Fargo eight dollars and twenty-cents, the original bet plus his winnings. Fargo took seven dollars out of the lad's palms and said, "Keep the rest, kid. You did a fine job."

"Thanks, a whole lot," Robert chirped, and crammed Fargo's tip in his pocket. "You want me to take care of your horse and all the other things I did last time?"

"Yep. Remember what you did?"

"Oh, yes, sir. I never forget."

Fargo paid him a dollar, then, rifle in hand, left.

After getting a room at the hotel, he left the Sharps in it and moseyed over to Keefer's Saloon.

Dulce Doll spotted him the instant he walked through the double doors. She came smiling to him. Curling an arm around his neck, she purred, "I see you came back to me." She pressed her body to him and kissed him openmouthed. As she pulled back, she whispered in his ear, "I want you, big man."

"Later," he muttered. "Right now I need a drink and a bath."

"You're always telling me later," she replied dejectedly. "We can drink up in my room. Before and after and during, if you like. And you don't need to bathe for me. I'm used to smelly men."

A blond-haired man, with a beard and mustache trimmed much like Fargo's, standing at the bar next to Fargo heard her. He nudged the big man's arm and in a friendly way said, "Best damn offer I've heard in a long time. If I were you, I'd take her up on it."

"I'll bet she would make the same offer to you," Fargo chuckled.

"No, I wouldn't," Dulce Doll pouted. She squeezed Fargo's crotch and said, "I want some of that."

Brushing her hand away, Fargo scanned the faces crowded in at the long bar, then at the bartenders, who were nowhere near him. He didn't want to wait for one of them to serve him. Glancing at Dulce Doll, he said, "Get a full bottle of bourbon and I'll follow you upstairs."

She patted his butt, then hurried away, grinning like a barracuda about to gobble up a tuna. The blond man laughed and remarked, "I've been standing here, waiting for a drink for ten minutes. You come in and in less than two get a whole bottle and a saloon girl to go with it."

Fargo threw him a wink, ambled to Dulce Doll, who was standing impatiently with one foot on the bottom step to the stairs. Going up the stairs, he asked, "Do you keep tabs on wagon trains heading west?"

"No, not really. Why do you ask? Wanting to join one?"

"No, but I'm heading that way. San Francisco."

"Harold keeps track of all the departures. Most all wagon masters come to the saloon. Harold talks to them and their men." She opened the first door they came to.

Fargo hadn't made it to the bed yet before Dulce started undoing his buttons. He stood there swilling from the bottle while she undressed him. He stood first on one foot then the other while she rode his shins to pull off his boots. The Levi's, and his under-drawers with them, came off last. Dulce Doll looked at his semihard length, then into his lake-blue eyes, and pursed her lips naughtily and tossed him a wink. "I knew from the bulge that you had a nice one hanging between your legs, big man. Now I've seen it!" She kicked her shoes off, turned her back to him, and suggested, "Why don't you undo the buttons on the back of my dress?"

Taking another swig of bourbon, Fargo grabbed the dress at her nape and yanked down. The small buttons popped off. She wiggled free of her dress, turned, and pressed her naked body to him. Between love bites on his broad shoulders she murmured, "Do you mind if I feel it in my mouth and throat?"

Before he could say, "Please do," she dropped to her knees and had the summit between her tightened lips. Fargo felt the lips draw his foreskin back, then her hot tongue lap the swelling, bulbous head, probe in its slit, then move down. Her hands clasped his buttock cheeks and pulled. She moaned joyously as she took in all of him, ceasing only when she reached the base. She had him in deeply now, plunged in the tender membrane of her throat where few men had been before. She took one hand off his buttock cheek to reach from behind and fondle his gonads as though milking them.

He entwined his fingers of his free hand in her hair and pulled her to her feet.

Breathlessly, she protested, "I wasn't through."

Fargo curled an arm around her waist and lifted her off her feet. Dulce Doll got his idea. She clamped those long, slender legs around his hips and dug her heels into his hard buttocks. He turned and backed her against the door. The head entered her hot, slickened opening. She gasped, "Oh, Jesus . . . oh, oh, Jesus . . . big man. You're driving me . . . cra-zeee!" Breathing hard, she clung to him, started pumping and whimpering her ecstasy, "Oh, yes, yes, yes—good, good. That's it, big man. Harder, more, more." Fargo thrust deeply and began gyrating. She gulped, "Damn, you're big. I've never had it so good."

Dulce Doll was moving her ass furiously now, gasping and moaning, trying to capture the last half-inch of the hard, slickened ramrod gliding in and out of her juicy tunnel. Her fingernails raked his muscular back as she bit him on the shoulder. She gasped, "Oh, Jesus . . . oh, Jesus, big man . . . I'm coming . . . I'm coming!" He felt her legs tighten around him, the heels dig in harder. She screamed her joy, "Aaaayyee!"

Fargo continued to power through the contracted inner membrane that squeezed his full length. Finally her contractions forced him to erupt. The lava-hot flow gushed into the nook, filled it, and overflowed through the widened opening. She kissed him hard, openmouthed, bit his lips, nibbled his earlobes, and sucked his shoulders.

Wringing wet with sweat, he carried her to the bed and laid her on it. Only then did she reluctantly release her leg lock on him. Out of breath, she said, "Damn, big man, that was a thrill. Best I ever had. Where did you learn how to screw so good?"

Fargo took a nip from the bottle first, then muttered, "There was this she-bear . . ."

Dulce found the strength to sit up and poke him on the chest.

He stepped to the side window and looked out. She commented, "You have a beautiful body, big man. So powerful and strong. I've never felt muscles big as yours before, and I do mean that muscle."

Fargo had heard it before. He knew what she would say next, and he was right. "Big man, before you leave this room, I want that much again. Please?"

He looked at the half-empty bottle, swigged from it again, then said, "I still need a bath, now more than before." Looking at her, he went on, "Get cleaned up and dress. I want you to introduce me to Harold Keefer."

"Aw, shit," she pouted. "You're not going to give it to me again. You've got your mind on wagon trains, not me. My pussy aches for you, big man. Please stretch it and make the hurt go away. Quit thinking about wagons and lay with me."

"No, Dulce. I'm finished for the night."

She got up and stepped to a small table that held a porcelain washbasin. She lifted a wet cloth from it and brought the cloth to Fargo. Cleaning him first, she said, "That'll be two dollars."

He chuckled. "You mean that'll be twenty-cents."

She parted her thighs and dragged the damp cloth

through her crotch, looked him in the eyes, and said, "Twenty-cents? Is that all I was worth?"

"No."

"Then, I don't understand, or is twenty-cents all you have in these Levi pockets?"

Pulling on his shirt, he explained, "I've already paid you a dollar and eighty cents."

She paused in putting on her dress and shot him a puzzled glance. "I don't recall any money changing hands."

"Robert, through Dennis, gave you five dollars to bet on the come line about three weeks ago. Remember?"

"Yes, I do. They normally get me to bet only one dollar. Five was unusual. So?"

"So, that five was mine. They won and you kept your part; the dollar eighty."

"So? That's what we agreed would be my part. I still don't understand."

Pulling on his underwear and Levi's, he replied, "Dulce, you didn't place that bet. You never once placed a bet for those two youngsters. You're like most whores I've known: generous to a fault. You made those kids think they won and gave them your hard-earned money."

Tears formed in Dulce Doll's eyes as she begged, "Don't tell them. Please, don't tell them. They're so young and adorable. Jesus, but I wish I were young again like them. I couldn't help myself, big man. Please, don't tell them. They would give back all the money and hate me forevermore." The tears burst and rolled down her cheeks.

Fargo felt ashamed of himself for exposing the truth. Pulling on his boots, he said, "I won't tell them. It's your money. You can do with it as you please. But, Dulce, they will grow up. One day they will walk up to that crap table thinking they will win every time, only to discover the truth. You are setting them up for a great fall. I suggest you—"

"I know, I know," she cried, and stopped him. "From now on, I'll place the damn bet, win or lose."

He dipped a hand into his pocket and brought out

Abigail's money. He counted off fifty dollars and handed it to Dulce Doll. When she looked at him questioningly, he muttered wryly. "Best screwing I ever had, Dulce. Worth every penny of it. You're far more exciting than the she-bear." He shot her a wink as he wiped the streak of tears off her cheek with his thumbs.

She smiled hugely. It went without saying that both of them knew damn well that Fargo's money was intended to reimburse her losses. He was sharing her generosity. She whispered, "You're a whore, too, big man. And I love you for it."

Nodding, he corrected through a tight grin, "Only when it's right, Dulce, only when it's right. Come on. Take me to Keefer."

Down in the smoke-filled saloon, she led him to the man running the crap game. She waited for a pause in the action, then tapped the man on the shoulder. He swirled and asked, "What is it, Doll? I'm busy." He glanced at Fargo.

Dulce began, "Mr.—" She looked at Fargo and frowned, "Say, what is your name, anyhow?"

"Skye Fargo. Some call me the Trailsman, outlaws and drifters call me a big son of a bitch." Smiling, he extended his hand to Keefer.

Gripping Fargo's hand firmly, Keefer said, "I've heard you called all three of those names, Fargo. It's my pleasure to finally meet you." He told one of his helpers to take his seat and watch things, then stood and suggested, "Why don't we move this conversation to my office, Fargo?"

Fargo nodded. He and Dulce Doll followed Keefer into his office on the ground floor, separated by the wall behind the crap table. Keefer sat in the chair behind his desk, gestured for Fargo and Dulce to take the plush, red-cushioned ones facing it. "What brings you to our fair city, Fargo? Pleasure or work?"

Dulce Doll grinned. "He's already given me the pleasure part."

"Received it back in kind," Fargo quickly added.

"Dulce tells me you keep track of wagon trains' departures."

Keefer nodded. "Yes, I do. As a matter of fact, I operate a wagon-train business from right here in this office. Most of the experienced wagon masters and I work closely together. I receive a small percentage of the gross amount westward-bound settlers pay for their services. I put the deals together. Are you interested in becoming a wagon master? You'd make a damn good one."

"No," Fargo began. "I'm looking for a pair of settlers, a man and his daughter. My customer has a good reason to believe they are headed west, to San Francisco."

"When did they leave?" Keefer inquired.

"Don't really know," Fargo answered. "But it had to be after mid-February."

Keefer grimaced. "Good God, man, do you not realize this is the nineteenth of April? Two and a half months later?"

"I said *after* mid-February," Fargo replied, easy-voiced. "They probably would have had to purchase a wagon and provision it. Then wait for a wagon train to assemble. Takes time. Am I not correct?"

Keefer rubbed his face, rolled his eyes back, obviously thinking, and finally said, "More than a dozen trains have left in the last two months. Not all led by wagon masters who work through me. I only work with the more experienced ones, men who know what they're doing. Decisive, no-nonsense men. Men who I can trust to perform."

"Then you're not a gambler?"

Keefer shook his head. "No, not really."

And that explained why Harold Keefer hadn't spotted the crooked dice. It did explain his honesty and fairness.

Keefer continued, "But we were discussing wagon trains and the men leading them. Let's see—two left between February fifteenth and the end of the month."

"On the twentieth," Dulce cut in. "I remember it well, because the night before, four settlers from that wagon train—men, of course—came here to get drunk. Sonny the bartender had to throw them out. They were raising too much hell. Pinched my butt black and blue. My bottom looked like ink spots for two weeks."

"Yes, it did," Keefer agreed. "Joe Conrad was in charge of that first one. The second one pulled out on the twenty-sixth. Doug Chambers led it. Four left in March. The first on the third. Then two almost back to back on the eleventh and fourteenth. Let's see now." Keefer paused to think on his fingers, then continued, "Three since the first of April, one on April Fool's Day. There were three wagon trains assembled that day. Only one was put together by me. All pulled out within hours of one another. My man is Shorty Stubblefield. Shorty told me the other two wagon masters were inexperienced, one leading for the first time. I think one of those other two trains was headed for Walla Walla. Anyhow, my other two in this month left on the sixth and nineteenth, respectively. That adds up to nine. Correct?"

Fargo nodded.

Keefer went on, "All led by my wagon masters. At the rate of thirteen miles a day, that would put the first one at or near, where?"

Fargo mentally made the extension and said, "They're on the North Platte in Sioux Territory below the Black Hills. About a month shy of South Pass."

Keefer nodded.

Dulce Doll mumbled, "How do you two think that fast? I can't."

The saloonkeeper suggested, "My man, if you burn leather, you can catch old man Joe Conrad before he reaches South Pass."

"Plenty of time," Fargo replied. "I'm in no big hurry. But there is a maniacal Cheyenne medicine man on the loose near South Pass. Joe had better watch for him."

"Oh?" Keefer said, frowning. "The same one who captured Lucinda Worthy a few years back?"

Nodding, Fargo told them about his rescue of Imogene Talbot.

Dulce Doll said, "That explains why you turned me down when you were in town earlier. You wanted her," she said cuttingly.

"No, I needed a bath," he smirked.

"You still do," she snorted.

"Say, didn't you kill four men over at Jack Turner's café when you were in town the last time?" Keefer said. "An Indian girl was involved? One of the men grabbed her?"

"Two," Fargo began. "Yes, I shot them." He glanced at Dulce and added, "Nobody touches a woman I'm with. Not without me putting up a fight." Looking back at Keefer, he went on to say, "They drew down on me. That called for a killing."

"Turner's been closed ever since," Keefer offered.

Fargo rose and extended his hand to the saloon-keeper.

Gripping it from over the desk, Keefer said, "Thanks for dropping in, Fargo. I've been wanting to meet you, and now I have. Hope my limited information is of some help to you."

"More than you realize," Fargo replied emphatically. Dulce Doll walked with him to the office door, where he paused to inquire about the fate of the two men who cheated Keefer. "I have to ask."

"Go on," Keefer answered.

"The two cheaters. Did you catch and hang them?"

"No. The bastards got away. I put a bounty on their heads. Five hundred for each, dead or alive, preferably dead."

Fargo ushered Dulce out into the hallway and shut the door. She embraced him and, stretching on tiptoes, kissed him, then she apologized. "Big man, I take back what I said in there. Especially the way I said it. I was being catty, wasn't I?"

He muttered, "What are you talking about?"

"You and that other woman. I'm sorry if I made you angry with me."

He touched a finger to her lips. "No apology necessary, Dulce. And you didn't offend me. Come on. Walk me to the swinging doors."

They walked side by side, Dulce next to the man standing at the bar. Passing the friendly blond chap, the fellow grabbed Dulce's wrist and pulled. She twisted free of Fargo's arm which was curled loosely around her hipline. The blond spun her into an arm-lock and pulled her body against his tightly. He chortled, "Baby doll, I want some free pussy." He glanced at Fargo. "You've had yours, now I want mine."

Dulce groaned painfully, "Stop. You're hurting my arm."

He applied pressure to the armlock and started for the stairs. Fargo stepped in front of them. Grim-jawed, Fargo said evenly, "The little lady told you to let her go. I suggest you do."

For a split second the only sound in the room came from the spinning wheel of fortune as it clacked over the dowels. Everybody in the saloon got still and watched the contest. Then, the men at the bar between them and the stairway, and those sitting at poker tables nearest the forming fight, rushed to make room for the combatants. Nobody wanted to get in the line of fire.

Holding his grip on Dulce's wrist high on her spine, the blond snarled through a twisted grin, "Get out of my way, cowboy. I suggest you'd better move if you don't want to get hurt."

Fargo watched the man's gun hand nudge open one side of his knee-length coat and expose a black gun belt and tied-to-the-thigh black holster holding a Smith & Wesson. Fargo realized he was facing a gun-slinger.

They drew at the same time.

Fargo was the faster. He didn't shoot for fear of hitting Dulce Doll. The man held her as a shield.

Fargo spun sideways, to his right, out of the line of fire.

The Smith & Wesson belched. The bullet whizzed past Fargo's head, splintering one of the steps.

Fargo slammed the barrel of his Colt into the Smith & Wesson, knocking it out of the gunslinger's hand.

The weapon clattered on the wooden floor beneath a poker table.

Releasing Dulce, the blond glanced to find his six-gun. In that instant Fargo holstered the Colt and powered a left into the gunman's gut. The man doubled over, groaning. Fargo followed up with a jaw-crunching uppercut. The fellow fell to the floor and began writhing, groaning loudly. Fargo pulled him erect, then drove his right fist into the man's nose and mouth. The nose cracked loud enough for those standing nearby to hear. Blood poured from the broken nose and spurted from the split lips. When Fargo let go, the man collapsed unconscious onto the floor.

Fargo said dryly to nobody in particular, "When this fool wakes up, tell him I'm no cowboy." Looking at Dulce, he nodded toward the double doors.

As they reached the doors, Dulce said, "He would have killed you. I'm not worth risking your life over."

"I felt honor-bound, Dulce. You were with me." He threw her an easy grin, then pushed through the swinging doors.

Dulce looked over them and watched him amble all the way to Ben Harper's Barber Shop and go inside. He might have heard her mutter, "What a man, what a man."

6

A dog barking in front of the hotel jarred Fargo's eyes open. For an instant he thought someone lurked in the dark shadows in his room. He slipped his gun hand beneath his pillow and gripped the Colt's handle. Then, sniffing the air, he got a whiff of lilacs and remembered he'd bathed with that fancy soap of Ben's last night. There wasn't anyone else in the room. He'd smelled himself. He laid the gun next to the pillow.

The big man stretched and yawned several times, then rolled off the bed and stepped to the window and looked out. Dawn was breaking. He glanced down. A clumsy, black-and-white-spotted puppy was worrying a big, scroungy yellow cat. The furry tabby was crouched in the middle of the street, and the yapping puppy was bouncing all around it. The cat flicked its bushy tail, warning the bothersome puppy to stay clear.

Ben Harper emerged from his shop, his arms laden with folded clothes. After learning Ben also took in washing and ironing, Fargo had the barber follow him to the hotel and wait for him to undress. Ben had offered overnight service. Now he was delivering. Fargo's clothes were in the stack. He leaned out the window and waved to catch Ben's attention.

Ben looked up at him and stepped into the street. While Ben was crossing it, the puppy lost all interest in the cat and started to intercept the barber. It made the mistake of coming within striking range of the cat. Both Fargo and Ben saw the angry cat pounce on the puppy's back, dig its sharp claws into flesh, then start chewing furiously on its victim's neck. The befuddled pain-stricken puppy cried loud as hell and tried shaking the cat from its back. When that failed, the puppy began rolling and twisting in the dirt. The cat finally let go and sauntered down the street as the puppy fled yapping in the opposite direction.

In a few moments Ben rapped on Fargo's door and announced his presence. Grinning, Fargo let him in. Ben said, "Ink Spots—that's the puppy-dog's name— just learned a lesson about messing with Lucifer— that's the tomcat's name—or any other mean tomcat. Your clothes are on top."

Getting them, Fargo suggested, "That tomcat has to be half-Cheyenne." Carrying them to the bed, he explained, "You never know what they're thinking, and you damn sure never know when they're going to pounce. Fifty cents?"

"If you please," Harper answered.

Fargo got four-bits off the bureau and handed it to him. "Thanks for the fast service, my friend. I'll remember where to bring them next time I'm in town."

Ben stepped out in the hall. Fargo was closing the door when Ben said, "Wait, Mr. Fargo."

From the urgent tone in the barber's voice, Fargo knew he didn't overlook any of his clothing. He pulled the door open and inquired, "Yes, Ben, what is it?"

"A fellow named Chad Stark took a bath right after you left. He had me tend to his busted nose, lips, and other cuts and bruises. Said a big son of a bitch jumped him when he wasn't looking. That big fellow by any chance you?"

"One and the same," Fargo answered, grim-jawed. "Only I hit him while looking straight into his eyes."

"Well, I want to warn you that he's looking for you."

"I'm leaving town in a few minutes. Chad Stark can look all he wants. I'll be gone."

"You coming back?"

"In a few months. Why?"

"Stark said he was gonna kill you. He's the kind that'll wait for you to come back. Like Ink Spots . . . Well, I'd watch my backside if I were you."

Fargo nodded and shut the door. He dismissed the blond from his mind and dressed. The freshly washed and ironed clothes felt and smelled good. Picking up his Sharps, he left.

En route to the livery he watched four sparrows dusting themselves in the dirt between hitching rails and walkways in front of shops. All was quiet, the air still, and the sky clear. Fargo yearned for the open country, the mountains and forests, anywhere but the city. To his way of thinking, cities were places to leave as fast as possible. "Too much grief," he muttered to the sparrows.

A sleepy-eyed Robert stood close to the front side of the livery as Fargo approached. Robert exchanged nods with him as Fargo entered the building. Seconds later he came in and hurried to Fargo. "Howdy, Mr. Fargo," he said in a tired voice.

Fargo saddled the Ovaro while Robert watched from a perch on the top board of the stall gate. "You ever gonna be back this way again, Mr. Fargo?" Robert yawned.

"Hell, kid, I don't know. Why?"

"Just asking. Want me to place another bet for you?"

Fargo flipped two-bits to him, saying, "Put it on the don't-come line. I have a feeling your winning streak is about to end. All do, you know."

After that Robert fell quiet until he and Fargo walked the trail-ready Ovaro outside and Fargo had his boot in the left stirrup. Then Robert told him, "A man asked me about you last night."

"Did he, now? Was he wearing a sort of long coat?" He eased on up into the saddle.

"Uh, huh. Had a bandage across his nose, too."

"Did he mention me by name?"

"No, sir. He asked if a big man kept his horse here. I told him the only big man around here lately was Mr. Fargo. Then I pointed out your stallion to him. He asked if you toted a Colt. I said you did. Then he gave me a nickel and left."

"He and I had a fight in the saloon last night," Fargo explained.

Kicking a horse apple into the street, Robert made a face and grumbled, "Shucks, I miss all the fun." Squinting an eye at Fargo, he added, "Beat the shit out of him, huh, Mr. Fargo?"

"I tried, Robert. Take care. I have to go now." He nudged the Ovaro to a walk.

Robert trotted alongside the stallion for a short distance to say, "I'd watch out for that guy if I was you, Mr. Fargo."

That made the second time this morning he'd heard the same warning. Maybe the youngster knew or saw something missed by the barber. Reining to a halt, he looked down at the boy and asked, "Why?"

"Not sure, Mr. Fargo. But I got a funny feeling when I was talking with him. Made my skin crawl, if you know the feeling. That's a mean man, Mr. Fargo. I get a creepy feeling ever' time I'm in a dangerous situation."

The kid's perceptive, Fargo thought. "Don't lose that feeling, Robert. One day it will save your life." He shook the reins, encouraging the pinto to proceed.

As he passed Keefer's Saloon, Dulce Doll came through the double doors, ran out, and stopped him. He saw that Dulce's face was bruised. Her left eye had been blackened. Cuts like those caused by bare knuckles were here and there. The woman appeared haggard, as though she hadn't slept a wink all night. "Oh, Fargo, I'd thought I'd missed catching you before you left town," she said in a distressed tone of voice.

He knew at once it had something to do with the blond-haired man. "Is Chad Stark giving you a problem?"

She looked up and down the street, then at him, and answered, "Yes. After you beat him up, he went to Ben Harper's place."

"I know that, Dulce. Ben told me."

"Then he came back to the saloon. He practically had to drag me to my room. I didn't want to go with him. He twisted my arm behind my back like he did before, and made me go. When we got inside the room, the guy went crazy. Real crazy. I mean to tell you that I was scared of that man. He was growling and snarling and hollering at me something fierce. I was trapped, Fargo, and didn't know what to do."

Fargo nodded grimly. Dulce went on with her horror story. "He ripped my dress off, flung me on the bed, and then undressed. He was rough on me, Fargo. It hurt. Now, I'm accustomed to abuse, okay—it goes with my job—but he went out of his way to hurt me."

"I get the picture, Dulce."

"No. That's only the beginning. Afterward, he wanted to know where you were. I told him I didn't know. That's when he started beating on me. He yanked my hair and twisted me off the bed and began slapping hard on my face. He said he'd make me tell where you were. You hadn't told me where you were staying, I didn't know. I wouldn't have told on you anyhow. Then he got his belt and whipped my butt till it bled."

Fargo's brow furrowed. The man was a maniac, he thought.

Tears welled in Dulce's eyes as she continued, "That's not all he did to me, Fargo. He also . . ."

The tears burst and streamed down her cheeks as Fargo watched her pull open the front of her dress to expose her breasts. Cruel burn marks and blisters dotted each of them. "Stark did that to you?" he grunted.

Pulling the front of her dress together, she nodded. "Yes, with his cigar. I'm ruined for at least a week, Fargo. Maybe forever." She started sobbing.

He dismounted and embraced her. Dulce clung to him, buried her face on his chest, and bawled. Fargo felt awful. He said, "I'm sorry, Dulce. I'm responsible for visiting all this misery on you. If it weren't for me, none of it would have happened. Somehow, I'll make it up to you. You can count on Chad Stark receiving my full wrath. Sooner or later his and my paths will cross again. When it does, I'll kill him this time, like I should have done last night."

She pulled back, looked into his chisel-boned face, and sobbed, "No. I'm not worth risking your life for. I'll be all right. Good as new. Please don't go looking for him. He's the kind that would see you coming and sneak behind you and shoot you in the back. He said he would. Fargo, the man is looking for you."

Dragging his thumbs on her wet cheeks, he muttered, "I'm on an urgent mission right now, but I'll come back and take care of Chad Stark." He dug Abigail Tuggle's money from his pocket, counted off an even hundred, and put it in her hand. "In the meantime, Dulce, this is the least I can do for inconveniencing you." When she shook her head and tried to hand back the money, he tightened her fingers around it and said, "No, Dulce, I want you to have it. Is it enough to tide you over till you recover?"

"More than enough," she sniffled.

He embraced her again and they kissed good-bye. Then he mounted up and rode away without looking back. Minutes later he headed west across the wheel-rutted assembly area. The wagon train he'd seen the evening before had already left. Not one Conestoga remained on the assembly site.

Fargo caught up with the slow-moving oxen teams soon enough, though. As he rode past the wagons, he scanned the people's faces, searching for one that resembled Abigail's description of her husband or daughter. He doubted they would be on a wagon train headed for Seattle, but he had to make sure. Passing the wagon master, Fargo nodded to him. For every step the sluggish oxen took, the Ovaro took three. Shortly, Fargo lost sight of the wagon train.

Fargo felt good. He was more or less in open country again. Dense greenery—huge oak trees mostly, and elm—formed a canopy over the much-used road on which he traveled, the beginning of the Oregon Trail. The road led past farms and through hamlets and villages and towns. Now and then farm fences—wood or stacked stones—emerged from the thick ground cover, marking property boundaries. They were necessary, of course, if for no other reason than to contain the farmer's cattle. The fencing—real or imaginary—stretched to the ever-lengthening and -expanding frontier and then, as though by magic, vanished altogether. At that point, a truly imaginary, irregular boundary line was drawn, separating the encroaching "civilization" from the wilderness, the Trailsman's home, his castle, his domain.

Riding through the canopy, he inhaled deeply of the plethora of springtime scents, and felt refreshed. He listened to and watched song birds: skittish cardinals, mockingbirds, sparrows by the dozens, and the unmistakable cooing of mourning doves. A barn owl hooted to him.

Working from the nine wagon trains' departure dates Keefer had told him, Fargo mentally projected their individual positions. For easy reference he assigned them numbers one through nine, with #1 being the farthest away. Joe Conrad was the wagon master. He concluded Joe's wagons had cleared Scottsbluff in western Nebraska Territory. His settlers would be viewing rolling plains and the oxen teams would be moving through grassy fields and meadows of renewed sage. In Wyoming Territory, which Joe was probably just now entering, Fargo knew the settlers were in for both a real treat and pure hell. First, they would see the majestic Rockies, then have to negotiate them . . . and that which lay beyond.

Train #2 would be on the north bank of the North Platte River, near Lewellen, Nebraska. As a matter of fact, five of the nine wagon trains, Fargo decided, were strung out in Nebraska Territory, three on the North Platte, one on the Platte itself, and #5 on the Little Blue near Endicott.

Train #6 surely had made it to where the Little Blue River branched in far northern Kansas Territory, just below the line. Trains #7 through #9 were still passing through Missouri. By now #7 was probably reprovisioning at Independence, #8 at Malta Bend on the Missouri, and #9, the closest to him, was in view of Hermann, some sixty-five miles from St. Louis. The Ovaro would overtake #9 soon, probably in four days.

Fargo didn't intend to wear his stallion out chasing after a pair of misguided souls. John and Hilary Tuggle would keep.

Sure death awaited everyone that left the wagon train, and he doubted they would, even if they were on one of the nine, or any of the others. It was always possible, he thought, that Abigail had sent him on a wild-goose chase. "It's her money in my pocket," he muttered sardonically under his breath. Fargo rode on.

At sunset he stopped and made camp a short distance beyond the hamlet of O'Fallon. He broke a low-hanging dead branch off a large oak and built a small fire in the grassy meadow where the pinto grazed. The light breeze, barely more than a zephyr, soon carried the aroma of coffee being brewed. Fargo spread his bedroll an arm's length from the coffeepot, then stretched his long frame on top of it and munched beef jerky while watching the first stars of the night twinkle on. After drinking most of the coffee, he undressed, got inside his bedroll, and went to sleep.

He was up before sunrise and rode until sunset. He spent the night camped next to a pond near a farm house. While bathing in the pond, the farmer appeared and invited the stranger to share dinner with his family. That evening Fargo ate good fried chicken, mashed potatoes, corn on the cob, biscuits, and gravy while the Ovaro had some oats in the farmer's barn. That night Fargo slept in the hayloft.

Sounds of the farmer chopping wood before dawn awakened the big man. He helped the farmer carry kindling to the house. The aroma of baking biscuits filled the kitchen. Mr. Tucker's wife stood at the stove, frying bacon and fixing scrambled eggs. Fargo ate a home-made breakfast for the first time since leaving the Fletchers' home outside Scottsbluff, Nebraska, when on his mission to rescue Imogene Talbot. Mrs. Tucker's food tasted delicious, and he told her so.

At sundown two days later Fargo came to a wagon train camped on the east bank of the Missouri River.

Womenfolk were busy preparing their evening meals. Smoke from the many cooking fires wafted lazily among trees on both sides of the river. Children ran among the wagons and trees, laughing and giggling. A ferry barge stood waiting at the near bank. Long sturdy ropes were secured to each end of the barge. Both ropes were tied to trunks of big oaks, one on the west bank of the river, the other on the east bank. Two teams of two mules each hauled the barge across the river. Two men were required to effect a crossing: one on each bank, to hitch and unhitch the teams to the ropes. They charged a ferry fee of twenty-five cents per wagon, a lucrative business what with all the west-bound traffic.

The wagon master and his men sat apart from the settlers. Seven men were huddled around a fire bigger than the others.

Fargo rode to them, dismounted, and introduced himself. A clean-shaven, husky, tall man—he looked as though he might be forty-five—invited Fargo to squat and have some trail coffee, then introduced himself. "Name's Clem Sanders. These are my men." Clem looked at each man as he stated their names. Some extended hands to Fargo, others simply nodded.

The introductions over, Fargo said, "I've met Harold Keefer."

"Dulce Doll, too?" one of the younger men muttered through an easy grin.

"Her, too," Fargo answered. He sipped from his tin cup, then looked at Clem and said, "I'm looking for a man and his daughter."

"You a lawman?" a man sitting on the far side of the fire asked.

Fargo shook his head and continued, "I have reason to believe they are on a wagon train heading west on the California Trail."

Shaking his head, the wagon master offered that there wasn't anybody by those names in his wagon train. "Any you men heard of them?" he questioned the others. They shook their heads. "Sorry, mister, that we couldn't be of help," Clem said wryly.

Fargo nodded, then suggested, "They might be traveling under other names."

Clem asked what they looked like. Fargo repeated Abigail's description of each. Clem said, "Hell, Fargo, I have more'n a dozen folks that looks like 'em." He glanced at the fellow who had asked Fargo if he was law and said, "Davey here keeps watch on a young woman and her papa that might be them."

"Mind if I take a look around?" Fargo asked.

"Help yourself," Clem replied.

"You want to introduce me to the might-be folks, Davey?" Fargo asked. He knew Davey wouldn't pass up the chance to visit his sweetie.

Davey made light of Fargo's request. Rising slowly, he muttered, "Aw, I suppose so. I gotta make my rounds anyhow."

All the others around the fire snickered. One said, "Davey Robertson, you ain't fooling nobody. You'd give your eye teeth to get close to Rebecca Peabody. I mean, real close."

"Shut your mouth, Obie, or I'll shut it for you," Davey threatened testily. "C'mon Mr. Fargo, I'll take you to their wagon."

They chatted while walking to the Peabody wagon. Fargo opened the conversation with a question. "What's Miss Peabody's father's name?"

"Uncle. She's an orphan. His name's Horace. Horace Peabody. He's from her daddy's side. You gonna take 'em back if they're the ones?"

"Bound and gagged if I have to."

"Oh, me. What did they do, anyhow?"

"Murdered two people." Fargo didn't want to talk about it.

"Rebecca didn't kill nobody," Davey said emphatically.

Fargo changed the subject. "Keefer said there's another wagon train ahead of this one."

"Yep. 'Bout a hundred thirty miles in front."

"Who's leading it?"

"R. D. McSpadden is the wagon master. Becky didn't do it," he repeated.

"We'll see," Fargo told him, and said nothing more until they were at the Peabody wagon, a Conestoga.

They found the uncle and niece eating red beans and corn bread. Fargo knew at once neither was his quarry. While Horace appeared the same age as John, and was balding, the sameness stopped right there. Horace stood taller than John. There were other differences, too. Horace was a frail, sickly-looking man, and he had a wart on his nose. Becky was redheaded, but her facial features and size didn't match Hilary's. Rebecca had an oval face and was petite.

Davey said, " 'Evening, Miss Becky, Mr. Peabody. Pardon me for interrupting your meal—that corn bread smells real good—but I want you to meet this man. Name's Skye Fargo."

Horace smiled and shook Fargo's hand.

Fargo explained, "I'm looking for a man and his daughter, John and Hilary Tuggle from Chicago. They are heading for San Francisco, same as you folks. But I see—"

Becky offered in a tiny voice, "Won't you and Davey sit for a spell and have some of my beans and corn bread?"

Davey didn't hesitate to accept the invitation. He sat. Fargo shook his head and said, "Ma'am, while those beans are making my mouth water, I'm afraid I have other folks to visit. Davey, here, will be glad to eat my portion." Fargo touched the brim of his hat, turned, and walked away.

He found five women with red hair, and three other men in various stages of balding. Both sexes were either too old or too young. He went back to get his horse.

Clem Sanders mused, "Well?"

"No," Fargo began. "I didn't think I'd find them this quick, anyhow."

"Davey makin' eyes at Rebecca again?"

Fargo grinned and nodded. "Yeah. She's fattening him up for the kill, feeding him red beans and corn pones." He eased into the saddle and said, "Take care, wagon master." He angled for the ferry and set the pinto to walk.

The ferry operator sat on a three-legged stool placed next to his fire, within easy reach of a big, blackened coffeepot that didn't look like it had ever seen soap and water. The man was short, wiry, had a long beard, and stunk to high heaven. His two mules stood nearby.

Fargo asked, "You and your helper want a fare?"

The fellow responded by turning toward the river and whistling loudly. Then he hollered, "Rider comin' across! Wake up, Byron."

Fargo watched Byron rise from the ground and start tying his end of the rope to the wagon tongue attached to his team's harness. Fargo paid the ferry operator two-bits. The man gestured for him to go aboard, then used the tree trunk as a winch to play out his rope. After swaying slightly when the current caught it, the barge straightened and Fargo's passage went without incident. As he led the Ovaro onto the bank, the ferry operator hitched his rope to the mules.

Fargo rode a short distance from the river to make his camp. He planned to be long gone before sunup, when the wagons would start coming across. He opened his bedroll so he could face west, then retired for the night. Lying there, he watched lightning flash in dark clouds that had gathered in the west.

Drifting off to sleep, he thought about how close he came to losing his life to Kills Fast. The medicine man would be far beyond the black clouds. Fargo wondered if Kills Fast was talking to him through the spirits in the clouds, lightning, and as-yet-unheard thunder.

If he was, Fargo decided, things seemed to hold an ominous promise of some sort for the Trailsman. Just what, he couldn't foretell. But it would be bad.

7

It stormed during the night, but dawn broke on clear skies. Fargo was up, had his morning coffee, and was astride the Ovaro before sunup. Knowing settlers heading west had to stay near water, hence, following the meandering Missouri River, he rode west by northwest to intercept R. D. McSpadden's wagon train. Shortly before sundown three days later, the shortcut paid off. Less than ten miles upstream of Lexington the rear wagon came into view.

Approaching at a gallop, Fargo saw a small boy and girl watching him through the scant opening in the canvas drawn tight at the back of the Conestoga. The little girl wore a yellow bonnet. When he waved to them, both ducked out of sight. Just as quick, curiosity got the better of them and they peered over the back end of the wagon. Fargo winked at them as he rode past.

Coming abreast of a stocky, bull-necked man riding in the van of the wagons, Fargo asked, "Are you R.D. McSpadden?"

The man spit a brown stream of tobacco as he scanned the black-and-white stallion, the Sharps and its saddle case, and Fargo's other gear, Finally he considered Fargo and grunted, "Mebbe. What you want him for?" He spat again.

"My name is Skye Fargo. Some call me the Trailsman. I'm looking—"

The man visibly relaxed. His eyes widened as he commenced to grin. "Wal, I'll be gawddamn," he began. "I've heard of you afore. Chief Washakie told me about you." Sticking his hand out to Fargo, he said, "Yep, I'm R.D. all right. What can I do for you?"

R.D. had a hard grip. Fargo liked him at once. "I'm looking for a couple of people, John and Hilary Tuggle. He's getting bald, she's redheaded."

"Fargo, I got forty-five people, counting the kids, in these fourteen wagons, and nair a one of 'em are growing through the hair on their head or has red hair. Now, you can see for yourself if you want to. I'll be halting the wagons outside Orick."

"I'll take your word for it. Mind if I make camp with you tonight?"

"Hell, I'd take it as an insult if you didn't. Widder Kate fixes meals for me and the boys. One more mouth won't make any difference to her. Kate fixes more'n we can eat, anyhow. You're invited by me."

Fargo nodded.

A farm house and a small general store set back about a sixteenth of a mile from the river came into view. The open space between the store and river showed signs of much use by wagons. Wheel ruts were everywhere.

McSpadden twisted in his saddle and shouted to the rear, "Awright, Jimmy Bob, park 'em, but not too close together. Four abreast and two at the rear." Turning to Fargo, R.D. explained, "Jimmy Bob, he's my lead helper."

Fargo angled off toward the store to wait for the wagons to be positioned and the teams of oxen unharnessed. An older man, grizzly as they come, and a young, underweight woman half the man's age sat in chairs leaned against the store front. She had dirty legs and wore a loose-fitting day dress that was torn in two places. He had a potbelly. A rope having frayed ends served as his belt. The fellow was bare-chested, and, like her, barefoot.

When Fargo got within hearing distance, she said, "My, my, big feller, ain't yew the purdy one, sittin' up there on that big ol' stallion."

"Hesh, your mouth, Wanda Sue," the man admonished. "I told you not to flirt with every stranger you see."

"Aw, Pa, I ain't flirtin'. I'm saying. Did I flirt with you, stranger,? Did I, huh?"

"No, ma'am," Fargo replied. "Leastwise, I didn't take it that way."

The old man snorted, "Bullshit." He rose, hitched up his pants, and sauntered toward the nearest wagon.

Wanda Sue came to Fargo. Running a finger over his leg, she looked at him and broke into a coquettish grin. Fargo knew what she would say before she spoke. Wanda Sue purred, "Why don't I show you the inside of our barn?"

She has a big itch between her two big toes, Fargo thought, and she's begging me to scratch it. He decided to put her off. Maybe she could get the itch scratched by one of R.D.'s boys or a settler. Fargo said, "See the inside of one barn, you've seen them all. Besides, I have work to do."

"No, you don't." Wanda Sue pouted. "You're not a settler, and you're not a wagon master or one of his boys, either. I happen to know all of R.D. McSpadden's boys. They're all married men. 'Sides, I've saw 'nuff pilgrims an' wagon-master kinds in my twenty-three years on the river to know you ain't neither. So how 'bout it, huh?"

He looked at her pa standing next to McSpadden. Nodding toward the two, Fargo said, "Want your pa to come looking for you?"

Wanda Sue took the question as a sign of encouragement. She leaned back against his leg and looked over her shoulder at him, then reached up and fondled his crotch. Fargo watched her eyes flare as she felt and squeezed.

He said, "Wanda Sue, I said I have other things to do!"

She persisted, seeming not to hear his last comment. Her fingers went to the buttons on his fly and tried to undo them.

Brazen hussy, Fargo thought. She was making him swell. He didn't want that to happen. He shifted in the saddle enough so that he moved away from the busy fingers. She rolled to face him, reached both hands up, worked them under his crotch, and captured his balls. "Gotcha now, big feller, and I ain't gonna let go till you say yes."

Her grip was so tight that he felt she would damage him permanently if he moved, especially if he tried to jerk free.

"Well, I do declare," she began. "Big feller, you got the biggest pair of balls I ever felt. Come with me to the barn?"

"Let go, Wanda Sue," he said, and gulped.

"Pa won't catch us. Right 'bout now he's asking R.D. if him and his boys want to play poker. Pa's a lousy cardplayer and R.D. knows it. They'll be up all night taking Pa's money." She let go of his gonads and started rubbing the insides of his thighs.

Fargo decided if she was as aggressive in the hay as she was standing there feeling him up, dirty leg girl or no, she might be exciting, at least interesting. He said, "Maybe later, Wanda Sue. Right now I have other business to tend to." He turned the Ovaro and rode toward the wagons.

He heard Wanda Sue sigh, then say, "I take what you just said as meaning a promise. Wantcha to know I make my men keep their promises."

Fargo found R.D. and Pa walking down between two rows of Conestogas. Coming alongside the two men, Fargo asked McSpadden, "Where are you and your men going to make camp? I'll put my horse out to graze near by."

Pa grunted, "Put him in the barn. That's where you'll be, anyhow."

R.D. said, "A short distance in front of the wagons, down by the river's edge. We'll be playing a few hands of draw after Widder Kate feeds us. You want to join us?"

Pa snorted, "He'll be too busy."

Pa's right, Fargo thought. He suspected the old man preferred to look the other way while his daughter favored men. The old man didn't want to see or hear.

So he played his cards while it was happening. Fargo said, "I'll hobble my horse by the river's edge." He turned the Ovaro and headed for the river.

After removing his saddle, bedroll, and other stuff, he hobbled the pinto and set him to graze. While he was doing it, a lanky man—Fargo guessed him to be thirty-five or so—rode up, dismounted, and said, "McSpadden mentioned I would find you here. Said for me to look for a big black-and-white stallion." He offered his hand to Fargo and added, "Name's Richard Ivy. Most everybody calls me Punch, though."

Fargo shook hands with him. "Glad to meet you, Punch."

Punch said, "Why don't we build a fire?"

In short order they dragged to the fire site dead tree limbs that had collected on the sandy point in the river's bend. Stacking the wood, Fargo inquired about Widow Kate, Wanda Sue and her pa, and how many men were in McSpadden's crew.

Punch addressed the question concerning Wanda Sue first. "I hear tell Wanda Sue's a hellcat. Don't know myself. Frankie—he was on R.D.'s crew a few years back—went to the barn with her. He came back at dawn the next morning and told us she wore him to a frazzle. Frankie, he looked like hell twice over. Claimed his pecker hurt like blazes."

Punch paused to chuckle, then continued. "Her pa can't do anything with his single-minded daughter's shenanigans. He has given up trying to control her. Wanda Sue's ma died giving birth to her. As for Kate, she's a honey bunch. You'll see. You are having some of her fixings with us?"

"Looking forward to it." Fargo struck a match and lighted twigs packed between the larger pieces of driftwood.

Punch went on, "McSpadden mention that we play cards after supper?"

"Yes, Wanda Sue told me her pa plays lousy draw."

Punch chuckled. Shaking his head slowly, he replied, "The old buzzard loses every hand. He draws to inside straights and never makes it. I've seen him holding

87

two pair and get bluffed. He keeps two hearts, for example, thinking he will draw three more. Stuff like that. Dumb. We take pity on him and let him win sometimes.

"There's four of us in McSpadden's crew. The other three are Leonard Murdock—one of the most honest men I've ever met—Dace Johansen, and Jim Bob Ross, R.D.'s right-hand man."

"I've met Jimmy Bob already. Do you know Shorty Stubblefield? I understand he's leading the wagon train that's ahead of this one."

"Now there's a character if I ever saw one," Punch began. "Shorty's a gruff no-nonsense kind of man. He doesn't take any backchat off anyone. Shorty's rough on his men, the settlers, and himself. He's led at least a dozen wagon trains west, either to Oregon or to San Francisco. Shorty has the reputation of getting the job done. He hasn't lost one person to the redskins. I like Shorty."

Two men walked up in time to hear the last comments. Hunkering next to the fire, one asked, "What's this about Shorty Stubblefield liking redskins?" He glanced at Fargo after making the statement.

Punch said, "Leonard, shake hands with—say, what's your name anyhow, big man?"

"Skye Fargo." He extended his hand to Leonard.

Leonard, a tall, rawboned man with piercing dark-blue eyes, broad shoulders, and a mop of curly, sandy-colored hair, pushed his cowboy hat back and said, "Skye Fargo? Aren't you the one they call the Trailsman?"

Fargo nodded.

The other fellow—Fargo guessed he might have seen his thirtieth birthday—shorter than Leonard by six inches, but more muscular, jumped into the conversation, saying, "I've heard tales about you, too. Didn't you go looking for, er, what's her name—Lulu Worthy?"

"Lucinda," Fargo corrected. "No, I didn't go look for her. She and other females had already been murdered by a Cheyenne medicine man. I went looking for him." He went on to tell them about his rescue of Imogene Talbot. They sat staring into the fire, mesmerized throughout the story. At the conclusion, Fargo warned, "Kills Fast is insane. He thirsts for young white females. He watches South Pass. I suggest you all do the same."

McSpadden, Jimmy Bob, and Pa sauntered up to the fire in time to catch part of Fargo's closing remarks. "What's this about South Pass and white women?"

"He was telling us about Lucinda Worthy," Punch answered.

Leonard added, "And how he saved another woman from the same Cheyenne medicine man who murdered her."

By now Fargo had guessed who Dace Johansen was. Johansen quickly added, "The Trailsman was saying we ought to be on the lookout for Kills Fast when we get to South Pass. The medicine man is crazy as a loon."

Pa didn't want to hear about a crazy man, especially a Cheyenne crazy man. He wanted to get on with the game. Fargo watched him pull a deck of cards from a hip pocket and start shuffling them.

"Not now," Punch told him. "After we eat."

Pa's expression changed from controlled excitement to near panic. His shoulders sagged. He stopped shuffling the cards. Sweeping his eyes around the circle of men, he snorted, "Aw, shit, fellers, yawl don't need to eat. C'mon, let's git started." He pleaded with his eyes as they went around the circle again.

"No, Shadrack," Punch replied, his voice laced with impatience. "We're tired and hungry. We want to rest a minute or two, then go eat. After we eat, we can play a few hands."

Shadrack jammed the cards back in his pocket and walked away, grumbling to himself.

Punch looked at Leonard. "Let the old coot win tonight." He wanted to say more, but a youngster ran up and interrupted.

The boy bent at the waist slightly and gasped for

air. The small boy and girl Fargo had seen earlier trotted to join and mimic the older boy.

"What is it, Les?" Punch asked the boy, gentleness in his tone.

The little girl answered breathlessly, "Ma told him to say your vittles are ready." She smiled winsomely as her big brown eyes cut to Fargo.

Fargo reckoned the widow was the fastest cook on the planet until Johansen explained, "She's having warmed-up leftover red beans and fresh-made corn bread."

Fargo cradled the little girl in one arm. She curled an arm partway around his neck and hung on while he carried her to her wagon. He asked, "What do they call you, missy?"

"Punkin," she answered in a tiny voice.

"Know where you're going, Punkin?"

"Franisco."

"How old are you?"

She held up three fingers and bent the fourth at the second joint.

Her ma was a fleshy woman, jolly and quick to giggle. Taking Punkin from Fargo, she said, "Now you young'uns don't get in these men's way. Hear me, Les?"

"Yessum, Ma," he said, and pulled the smaller boy to him.

Fargo buttered and ate a slice of corn bread before he partook of the beans. None of the men spoke while eating. Fargo wondered why the widow was going west.

As though reading his mind, she giggled. "Me and the kids are stopping in Carson Valley. Bill Smedley, a man I've never met, and I are going to get married. Bill's a miner. He sent for us. Paid all the expenses, didn't he, Mr. McSpadden?"

R.D. didn't look up from his bowl of beans when he nodded.

Fargo reckoned the widow would do well with the miner in Carson Valley. It would be a hard life, yes, but her gift of laughter would make the difference.

Out of the corner of his eyes he noticed Wanda Sue lurking in the fringes of firelight cast by the fire behind the adjacent wagon. She eyed him like a starving fox about to catch a trapped hen.

McSpadden had obviously seen her, too. He muttered, "Trailsman, I think somebody is looking for you."

All the other men's eyes kicked up from their beans to see who. They quickly spotted Wanda Sue, then, satisfied that R.D. meant her, resumed eating. Fargo's bowl was empty. He wiped his lips, rose, and mumbled, "Think I'll take a long walk. Don't wait up for me."

The widow giggled. Two of the men chuckled. Fargo patted Punkin on the head, then ambled toward the hellcat.

Leading him to the barn, she lamented, "My goodness gracious, sakes alike, big feller, what took you so long? Dang!"

"Well, I'm here now."

Wanda Sue hung on to his gun belt, as though he might try to cut and run.

The barn was behind and off to the right of the small house. Both were ramshackle structures: wide gaps between the planks, split boards, some planks missing altogether. One of the posts holding up the roof of the front porch of the house was broken—knee-bent—and the roof sagged badly. Fargo couldn't imagine what was holding it up. The porch roof appeared ready to collapse with the slightest jolt.

The moonlit barn didn't look to be in any better shape. Fargo had been in pitiful-looking barns, but this one appeared dangerous; it leaned severely. Skinny tree trunks propped the damn thing up.

A hen house that Fargo reckoned was more livable than the tumbledown house or the rickety barn stood less than a stone's throw away directly behind the house. Pigs grunted in their pen behind the hen house.

As they approached the barn door, several pigs started squealing and the hens in their house started squawking. The screen door at the back of the house squeaked open. Shadrack, armed with a shotgun, ran out in the yard a few paces, stopped, and raised the double-barreled weapon. The first blast of shot tore into the hen house. The retort was all it took for the already broken post to give way. The porch roof fell. A great cloud of dust blossomed all around the debris. Shadrack jumped, swung, and fired the other barrel. That pattern of shot raked one of the posts propping up the barn. Fargo heard the tree trunk slowly begin splintering. The barn trembled. The trunk snapped. The barn tilted even further, then grabbed and held.

Shadrack rushed to the front of the house. Fargo saw a fox run out of the hen house. The terrified hen it had captured beat its wings on the ground and squawked most loudly.

Wanda Sue jerked the barn door open and yanked Fargo inside.

Moonlight spilled through wide cracks in the side of the barn and through holes in the roof. Coils of rope hung from nails, as did rusty bow saws, shells of lanterns, and rags. Two sledgehammers leaned against one wall. So did a couple of shovels and one pick. Wanda Sue guided him around a freestanding, large, circular whetstone to a pile of hay in the back of the barn. Thumbing off the shoulder straps of her day dress, she said, "Well, I swear, big feller, don't just stand there. Get naked." The day dress fell to her bare feet.

A ray of bright moonlight coming through a crack highlighted a narrow strip down the full length of her skinny body. Fargo looked at her plum-sized breasts first. The areolae covered practically all of both. Big nipples stood at attention. Well, he thought, plums are one of my favorite fruits.

His gaze moved down her bony rib cage, across the flat belly, to the sparse patch of flat-growing pubic hair. The woman was so lean that her Venus mound protruded.

She said testily, "Well, what're you waiting for?"

He removed his gun belt slowly and lowered it to the dirt. That wasn't fast enough for Wanda Sue.

Loosening his belt buckle, she said, "I can see you're the bashful kind. Lie down. I'll undress you. You can pinch my titties while I do." She motioned for him to lie on the pile of hay.

She straddled his shins to pull off his boots and socks. As she tugged and grunted, he stared at the widest buttock crack and the hardest cheeks he ever saw. The cheeks barely jiggled with every vigorous move she made while getting the boots off. Twice he glimpsed her glistening crotch. Both times the legs parted, exposing raw, juice-covered membrane. The boots came off.

Wanda Sue knelt beside his waist to take his pants and underdrawers off. She said, "I like undressing a man. The pants are the best part."

Raising his hips a tad to make it easier for her, he pulled his shirt off. Opening his fly, she repeated, "C'mon, big feller, pinch my titties. I promise not to holler."

He reached and tweaked both nipples.

She moaned, "Pull on 'em."

As he gripped both plums and pulled on them, he felt his Levi's and underwear being yanked down to his knees. One of her hands instantly went to his scrotum, the other gripped his hardening member. Wanda Sue gasped, "Dang, you got a nice, big one." She started massaging the bag, stroking the staff. "Mind if I taste it?" she mumbled.

He reached down and pulled the rest of his clothing off. Her stringy, straw-blond hair aroused his groin when she bent to feed his manhood between her lips. Wanda Sue didn't fool around. The lips met his base in one swift plunge. Moaning, she started bobbing and rolling her head furiously. Her lips tightened on each downward thrust, relaxed coming up to the swollen head. As she came up, she gasped, "Goddamn . . . that's good!"

He felt her kiss his balls, then her lips suck the bag into her mouth. Nursing on it, she mewed, "Them two balls rolling 'round in there are the biggest I ever felt."

Fargo could not stand the sensation any longer. That good feeling, coupled with her tight stroking grip on his throbbing length, would cause a premature eruption, and he didn't want that to happen. He pulled her head up. Looking at him questioningly, the little hellcat quipped, "Why did you make me quit sucking? Did I hurt you or something?"

"No," he muttered. "I was ready to explode."

Wanda Sue smiled as she straddled his waist. His pulsating manliness rode up her flat belly. Rubbing the tender underside of his large poker, she cooed, "Bite my titties, big feller. Try to suck 'em off. Suck till they're raw." She collapsed forward and stuck the left one into his mouth.

Fargo took in the whole plum. She started squirming, pressed her chest even tighter to his lips, and moaned joyously, "Oh, boy . . . oh, boy! That feels so good . . . so dang good. Bite me, please . . . bite me. Suck harder, too!"

When he nibbled the nipple, she gasped, "That's it . . . that's it. Suck it off."

He moved to the left breast, swished his tongue around the areola and nipple several times, then sucked in the firm mound. Trembling with excitement, she writhed, dragging the nipples across his lips so he could favor first one, then the other. As she did, she raised her hips higher and higher until the ruby-red crest of his towering roundness touched her heated, well-slickened lower lips.

Wanda Sue gasped, "Oh, my God . . . oh, my God! That big head down there . . . it feels so good to me." She squatted hard. He went in deeply. She screamed her delight. "Aaaugh! I gotcha now! Go deeper, big feller!"

When he thrust as hard as he could, her fingernails dug into his nape to give her leverage. She started romping fiercely, riding high on his hard ramrod, which was giving her so much pleasure. Her hips moved furiously, as though a long sexual drought was finally over, as though it might return suddenly. Wanda Sue bucked, twisted, bore down hard, and gyrated swiftly on the long, hard peg of blood-swollen flesh, all the while moaning and gasping, whimpering and murmuring her unbridled ecstasy. The woman was tireless. It went on and on unbelievably long. They were both bathed in sweat. She bit him on the ears, shoulders, chest, and face, raked him with her finger-nails until he was crisscrossed with red ribbons of blood.

Fargo grabbed her hard butt and pulled down, more to slow her wild antics than anything else. The net effect of his downward pull was such that Wanda Sue commenced gulping. She yelled, "I'm coming, I'm coming! Oh God, yes . . . yes, yes, I'm coming!" She was frantic now, screaming, "Oh! Oh! It feels so . . . good!"

He erupted deep inside her hot tunnel. With her eyes shut tightly, she grabbed his biceps and moaned. "Oh, that's so hot. Don't stop. Please, don't. Not now. Not when I'm in heaven."

But, thoroughly exhausted, he softened and slipped out. She put it back in, set her hips to pumping slowly, rhythmically, and whispered, "Dang, even though it is limber, it still feels good in there."

The woman doesn't know when to give up, Fargo thought, but said, "It's tired, Wanda Sue, and so am I."

She mumbled, "We'll let it rest a spell, then go at it again." She rolled to one side. It fell out. She lifted and bounced his scrotum with two fingers, and asked, "Want me to suck your balls again?"

"No. I just want to lie here and catch my breath."

As soon as he closed his eyes, he felt her lips on his summit. She murmured. "I want to get the last drop out of you. I'll suck that bag plumb-dry." Wanda Sue started sucking.

Fargo had to take her by the hair and pull her off him.

She chastised, "Why did you do that? I like to taste it."

He flopped onto his abdomen to deny her eager fingers and willing mouth.

"Why did you turn over? I wasn't hurting you none." She slapped his butt, sighed disgustedly.

"Later, Wanda Sue. Maybe."

"Aw, shit. You're going to sleep, aren't you? Just roll over and go to sleep. Men always do that, just when I'm all juicy and ready."

He had to get her mind off it, if but only a few minutes. He remembered what a Texas whore once told him: "The single best thing a woman enjoys best is screwing. The next best is getting a man to talk to her." Well, he thought, I've screwed her. He said, "Let's talk."

"About what? I don't talk when I'm fucking."

"You aren't doing it now."

"But I want to."

Wanda Sue was as persistent about engaging in sex as her father was about playing cards. Both were hopeless addicts. Fargo chose a nonrecreational subject. "When did the last wagon train pass this way?"

"Two days ago. The one before it left five days ago. Why?" She snuggled up to his side. He felt her right arm and leg on his back and butt.

"Was there a redheaded woman about your age on either of them?" He went on to describe Hilary.

"I didn't see anyone like that. Harley Skaggs was here, though. Harley, he's the wagon master of the one that left five days ago. I fucked him. You don't mind, do you? Huh, big feller?"

"Not in the least."

"Some do, you know. They think they own me. Most don't, though. They just screw me and leave me. I like it that way."

The little hellcat had a good thing going, Fargo thought. She had a hot crotch that lay directly in the path of plenty of men who would stoke it.

Wanda Sue continued, "Harley, he ain't got much, though. His ain't nowhere as big or long as yours." She squeezed his butt. "Now that I think on it, his was little like the first man that stuck his in me. I was a scrawny fourteen-year-old girl back then. Ugly as mud fence, too. That sorry, good-for-nothing bastard got my little ass right here in this very barn. When he stuck his little pee-pee in me, it felt like a big pole. I hollered. I screamed. I told him to take it and leave me be, that he was splitting me wide open and ruining me for life. Oh, but it hurt.

"Know what he did? No? Then I'll tell you. The son of a bitch just laughed. He told me I had a tight pussy and he was going to loosen it up."

"Where was your pa during all this?"

"Pa was scared to death of him. Didn't come out to see why I was hollering or anything. That guy kept me buck-naked for three nights in this here ol' barn. He took turns going in my three holes at least twice every night. I was raw and sore as hell for a week after he got through stretching me. Could hardly walk.

"He even came in my mouth and made me swallow it. Oh, I gagged, choked, and puked my guts out, all right. That is, till he touched the burning end of his cheroot to my ass. That's when I learned to gulp it down."

Already guessing the answer, Fargo asked, "Who did this to you?"

"Chad Stark."

8

A loud noise, like somebody strangling on a chicken bone, jarred Fargo's eyes open. He was fully awake and mentally alert instantly. Instinctively his gun hand moved to his holstered Colt lying on the ground beside him. The raucous sound erupted again. This time he realized it came from a young rooster learning how to crow the sun up. The bird was simply having trouble with the tune, rhythm, and correct order of its cockle-do-dee-do. Fargo relaxed his grip on the Colt's handle.

The glow from morning cooking fires down at the wagons filtered through the many cracks in the barn and painted its interior eerie yellow. He looked at Wanda Sue. She lay flat on her back, snoring softly. When Fargo stretched and yawned, her sleepy fingers fumbled to find his aching member. He lowered his left hand and gently stopped the fingers from any further encroachment. Fargo didn't dare awaken her.

Wanda Sue had forcibly romped him three more times during the night, then begged for a fourth. The energetic little spitfire simply did not give up, didn't wind down. She would get up, fetch a rag hanging on one of the nails, drag it through her crotch, and be ready to go again. The dull ache in his member resulted from rubbing at least a mile against her bony Venus' mound. The fact that it was well-lubricated made no difference. Her groove was dangerous.

The young cock tried again—off-key, of course— and failed. The rooster apparently had its beak pointed at a gap left by a missing board. The raspy, croaking crowing blasted through the opening and reverberated off the walls. Fargo had to get out of the echo chamber. He dressed hurriedly, groped his way around the huge whetstone, and squeezed his big frame out the partly opened barn door.

He paused to take a few breaths of the fresh morning air. As he did, he looked toward the wagons. Men and older boys worked in silence as they went about harnessing their teams of oxen. He glanced at the star-filled sky. The rooster began its strangling crow yet another time. Like Wanda Sue, the rooster had no intention of giving up. Fargo looked toward the horrible sound. He barely made out the strutting chicken's shape on the top rail of the pigpen.

Before the rooster was halfway through its crowing, the screen at the rear of the house banged open. Fargo saw the dark form of the double-barreled shotgun poke out. Pa apparently pulled both triggers at the same time. The explosion shook the barn. Flames leapt from the barrels. The young rooster—guts, feathers, and all—simply vanished from the rail. The pigs started grunting and squealing loudly. Fargo watched the tilted barn split down its length. Its low side crashed to the ground and raised a great cloud of dust. The other half wavered momentarily, then caught and stayed up. Fargo looked at the woman sprawled on the pile of hay. The hellcat had slept through all of it.

He went to the wagons and found McSpadden. The man was busy, so Fargo made it brief. "I'm leaving now. Glad to have met you." They shook hands. Fargo turned to leave. After taking two strides, he turned back and said, "Wanda Sue mentioned a wagon master named Harley Skaggs. Said he was ahead of Stubblefield. Do you know anything about the man?"

Grimacing, R.D. shook his head, then said, "Skaggs's a greenhorn. First wagons he ever took west. Yeah, I know the blowhard. And his two men. Neither of them is dry behind the ears. Kids acting like men." He shook his head again, then continued the denouncement. "Harley Skaggs's a mule-skinner by trade, and a sorry one at that. He never set foot west of Scottsbluff. Those men of his . . . Hell, they ain't been on this side of the Mississippi till now. I wouldn't want to be on those wagons he's leading. Nosiree, I wouldn't."

"How far ahead of Stubblefield is Skaggs?"

"Lessee . . . by now Shorty's left Kansas City. Skaggs's ahead of him by three days. So his wagons are still hugging the Kansas River, on the far side of Topeka."

Fargo nodded and left. He went to his stallion and made him ready for the trail. Easing up into the saddle, he glanced at the gray sky. It promised to be a long hot day. Between wrestling with Wanda Sue all night and then suffering the noisy rooster, he had gotten precious little shut-eye. He encouraged the Ovaro into a slow walk and left the wagons, Shadrack's deadly shotgun, sleeping Wanda Sue, and pigs and dead rooster far behind.

About five miles upstream it occurred to him that Wanda Sue hadn't answered his query about Hilary Tuggle being on one of Stubblefield's or Skaggs' wagons. Not that it mattered, for he intended to catch up with both in short order. He quickened the Ovaro's pace and rode at a gallop, following the north bank of the Missouri. He cleared Kansas City before dark and continued to Edwardsville, Kansas, where he stopped for the night to bathe in the river.

He was back in the saddle at daybreak and continued at the accelerated pace, walking the stallion for about a mile, changing into a gallop for the next. By midafternoon, the town of Lawrence appeared on the horizon. In less than an hour he entered the town and saw Conestogas parked on the main street. Most of the settlers were on the ground, inspecting wheels and other hardware, securing ropes that had worked loose, or standing in small groups talking. As he rode by, he looked for John or Hilary. He stopped twice, once to wait for a red-haired woman about Hilary's size and build to turn toward him, once to get a better look at a balding man that fit the description of John. Neither was his quarry.

Fargo counted ten wagons. Several men were changing a broken right front wheel on the lead Conestoga. He reined to a halt, dismounted, and added his strength to theirs. Two men carried the damaged wheel to a wagon-repair shop while Fargo and the others put on a spare. Fargo knew right off that the eldest in the group of men was Shorty Stubblefield.

Shorty took control of the situation, bellowing orders right and left in a whiskey voice, replete with expletives. "Goddamn, Jake, can't you lift any higher than that? Shit, why won't it go on? Feeney, slap some lard on that axle."

And so it went until the spare wheel was in place. Only then did the leathery-faced Stubblefield acknowledge Fargo. Shaking the big man's hand, Shorty said, "Thanks, pardner, for helping get the bastard on."

"The lard and the grunting did it," Fargo replied. "You're Shorty Stubblefield, aren't you?"

"Yep. You and I met before? Can't place you if we did."

"Maybe. My name's Skye Fargo. You might have seen me back in St. Louis. Harold Keefer told me where to find you. So did R. D. McSpadden two days ago."

"How's McSpadden doing?"

"I caught up with him at Orick. He's doing all right."

Shorty grunted, nodded, then asked, "So, Mr. Fargo, what can I do for you? You do want something, don't you? Show you the way to Cal-ee-forn-i-ay? That it?"

Fargo grinned. "No, I think I can find the place all by myself. I'm looking for a man and his daughter." He went on to describe them.

Shaking his head slowly, Shorty answered, "No. Don't think so. I got two redheaded females and three bald-headed men, but they're younger than you say. And I know I ain't got nobody named Tuggle on this wagon train. You might check the wagons ahead of me . . . if you can catch that sorry son of a bitch what calls hisself a wagon master."

"Harley Skaggs?"

Shorty's eyes kicked up. "You know him?"

"No, but I've heard about him. McSpadden told me."

Shorty returned to Fargo's problem. "Normally, I don't pay any attention to the color of folk's hair, or if they have any. Now, there were three wagon trains making up at the same time back in St. Louie. Mine and two others. Anyhow, there was a redheaded woman that I remembered 'cause the bitch was a troublemaker. Hotheaded, testy female, she was."

Fargo sensed he was closer to Hilary than he imagined. "Is the woman on Skaggs' train?"

"Either his or the other one. Skaggs is headed for California, the other for Oregon. Both are in front of me. Skaggs' by three days or so, the other by six." Shorty nodded toward the saloon nearby and suggested, "Say, why don't we step out of the sun to continue this conversation? I'll buy you the first drink for giving us a hand with that wheel."

"Don't mind if I do." Fargo led his stallion to a hitching rail in front of the saloon.

Shorty watched as Fargo loose-reined the pinto next to four saddled horses. "Mighty fine Ovaro you have there, Mr. Fargo. Strong withers and hind-quarters. Had him long?"

"Caught him coming out of his mama." He stroked the pinto's powerful neck, then followed Shorty through the swinging doors.

Six men—Fargo reckoned they were settlers off Stubblefield's wagons—stood drinking beer at the bar. Four wranglers and a saloon girl occupied a table by the front windows. Fargo and Shorty joined those at the bar. Shorty asked, "What's your poison, Mr. Fargo?"

"Bourbon."

Shorty broke a grin and slapped him on the back. "Shit, I reckoned I liked you on first look." He told the bartender, "Two glasses of bourbon, Dooley, if you please." While Dooley poured, Shorty looked at the settlers' reflections in the mirror behind the bar and said, "Drink your fill, men. It's a long, hot trail that leads to Fort Kearney."

Fargo heard a chair at the table be scooted back. He glanced at the mirror and saw one of the cowhands stand. Their eyes met as the cowboy came toward Fargo. He turned to face the fellow.

The wrangler said, "Did I hear your friend call you Fargo?"

Fargo nodded.

"I'm not one to butt into two men's private business," the cowhand began, "but there was a man looking for you in here yesterday. He asked us if we had seen a big man by the name of Fargo. He said he would be riding a black-and-white pinto. We watched you loose-rein just such a horse."

"Go on," Fargo said, now a tad curious to know more.

"Like I said, I'm not one to butt in. That man told us he was out to kill you. If he was looking to kill you in a fair fight, that would be another matter. But he isn't. Now, I know a dry-gulcher when I see and hear one. I don't cotton to shooting a man in the back, so that's the only reason I'm warning you."

"What's your name."

"Ward Hooker. Why?"

"Well, Ward, I want to buy you a drink for warning me. What'll it be?"

"I'm drinking whiskey." Ward bellied up to the bar.

Fargo caught the bartender's attention, ordered a glass of his best whiskey for Hooker, then looked at the cowpoke's reflection and asked, "What was the man's name?"

"Didn't say."

The bartender had eavesdropped their conversation. He said, "Chad something or other. I didn't catch his last name. But what Ward told you was right. He's a bad one. Molly took him to her room out back. Maybe he told her more." He shouted to those at the table, "Molly, come here a minute."

Molly sauntered up to the bar. "What is it, Dooley?" She glanced at Fargo and Ward Hooker.

Fargo said, "Yesterday you had a customer named Chad Stark. Tell me—"

"That slimy bastard," Molly blurted. "Whatcha want to hear about him? I can tell you plenty about that rotten son of a bitch."

"My name's Skye Fargo. Did he say why he was looking for me?"

"He said you sneaked up behind him and tried to choke him to death. Big man like you, I'm surprised you'd do such a thing. Did you?"

"No, Molly. Chad twisted the truth when he told you that. He had a gun pointed straight at me and used a saloon girl as a shield. I beat him up, all right, but didn't choke him. Guess I should have. Did he hurt you?"

"I should say he did." Molly raised the hem of her dress up above her thighs and parted them. On the inside of her left thigh was a nasty-looking blister. She explained, "He had me on my hands and knees, poking in from behind. Said I wasn't moving my ass fast enough. The louse burned me with his cigar." Molly released the hemline.

"You were lucky," Fargo muttered. "I know of two women Chad did worse things to. I should have killed the man when I had the chance."

Ward Hooker had nipped on his whiskey while Fargo and Molly conversed. Now he spoke. "I haven't seen him in town today. Has he been in here, Dooley?"

Molly answered, "Stark left town right after he got through with me."

"When was that?" Fargo inquired.

"After dark. I'd say about eight o'clock. Are you going after him? Say yes."

Fargo shook his head. "I don't know which way he went. Do any of you?"

"You bet," Molly cried. "He rode for Fort Kearney."

"Did he tell you that?" Fargo quizzed.

"That's what he said," Molly began. " 'Sugar doll, the big son of a bitch is ahead of me,' he said. 'I'm going to Kearney. If he isn't there, then I'll follow the Platte till I find him.' Those were his very words."

Fargo calculated that Chad had a twenty-hour lead on him. He commented, "I'm going to Kearney. I hope he's still there when I arrive."

"If you get there," Ward offered sardonically.

Shorty added, "He may plug you on the way. Hell, for all you know he ain't even left town."

Ward said, "Gotta go back to my drinking pardners. I hope everything works out for you, Fargo." Ward downed the last of his whiskey, then went to his table and sat.

Fargo said, "I better be getting on down the trail." He turned to Stubblefield. "Thanks for the drink, Shorty."

Shorty walked outside with him. He watched Fargo ease up into the saddle, then said, "I wouldn't want to be in your boots for anything."

Shrugging, Fargo replied, "Cowards and sneaks are no problem. It's the ones who look you in the eye and smile that you have to worry about. So long, Shorty. By the way, Cheyenne are raising hell at South Pass. Watch for them. See you later, my friend." He wheeled the Ovaro and eased him into a slow walk.

Lawrence slid out of view. After three hours of following wagon-wheel ruts carved in the loose soil near the river, Fargo made camp. While drinking coffee, he wondered what the new day would bring. Chad? Fargo doubted he would run into him, although a chance meeting was possible. After all, Chad had it fixed in his mind that Fargo was in front of him and was riding hard for Ft. Kearney. Fargo quit thinking about Chad Stark, trying to outguess the man's movements. He still had six of Keefer's wagon trains to search, plus Skaggs', and God only knew how many others strung out between Shorty Stubblefield's and Joe Conrad's.

For an instant he considered abandoning the normal route of the California Trail, bypass Ft. Kearney—hence, Chad—altogether, and ride straight as a Cheyenne arrow for South Pass to intercept Joe. If John and Hilary weren't on one of Joe's wagons, he told himself, then he would backtrack until he found them. But he discarded that idea almost as quickly as it had formed. He was less than a day's ride away from wagon train #4. Two more days and he would overtake Skaggs'. Being so close, he reckoned it best to check those two wagon trains first. Those were the big man's final thoughts before he drifted into sleep looking at the stars.

He awakened shorty before dawn. A light breeze carried a chill. Low-hanging, moisture-laden clouds had moved in from the west during the night. They were the kind of clouds that promised rain. Fargo added twigs to his dormant camp fire to warm up his coffeepot, then went to the river to wash up. As he washed his face, his thoughts returned to Stark. The man was a bother, out to get himself killed. Fargo decided he would make it a point to confront Chad Stark face-to-face in Kearney and have it out with the man once and for all. He didn't intend to keep looking over his shoulder to spot the man. "If he's in Kearney," he mumbled.

Fargo had his morning coffee, rinsed the coffeepot and his tin cup in the river, then made the stallion ready for the trail. Getting into the saddle, he looked at the foreboding sky. Ugly clouds churned overhead. The wind had picked up speed, too. He coaxed the pinto into a walk; then, after giving the stallion a moment to work the night's sleep out of his muscles, he stretched his gait into a lope.

The wind stiffened as he approached Topeka. Entering town, a driving rain smacked the big man in the face. He dismounted and put on his poncho, then rode through Topeka without further pause. He came to the wagons less than ten miles upstream. They were bogged down in mud near Willard. Riding past the long column, he counted sixteen wagons, all Conestogas. Most everybody had taken shelter inside the canvas-topped wagons. The few who hadn't sat glum-faced in their drivers' seats. Rainwater pelted them, cascaded from the brims of their hats. The wagon master and his four men were squatted beside their horses, their hats and ponchos providing little relief from the torrential, wind-whipped downpour.

Fargo called out, "Which of you is the wagon master?"

One of them stood and said, "I am."

Fargo dismounted and went to him. "My name is Skye Fargo."

"I've heard of you. Mine is Jude Crowley. What brings you out in this weather, Trailsman?"

Fargo told him.

Jude replied, "There isn't anybody by those names in these wagons."

Fargo hadn't expected John and Hilary to go by their own names. He'd taken a shot and missed. He described the two.

"I have two people who more or less fit that description," Jude told him. "Bob Crowder and his daughter, Lorelei. I'll introduce you to them."

Fargo followed Jude to the sixth wagon in the line. Jude called, "Bob, want you to meet a man. You, too, Miss Lorelei. Poke your heads out."

The front of the canvas parted. A bald-headed man peered out. Fargo knew at once Bob Crowder wasn't his man. He waited to see the daughter. A flaming-red-haired girl of about twenty appeared beside her father. Jude looked at Fargo.

Fargo said, "Sorry to have bothered you folks. I'm looking for somebody and thought you might be them." He turned to Jude and shook his head.

Walking back to the horses, Jude volunteered, "Now I know for a fact that there's a redheaded woman on the wagon train just ahead of us. Same color of hair as Lorelei's. However, the sameness stops there. Lorelei doesn't hold a candle to her when it comes to rowdiness. Jessie will fight at the drop of a hat."

Abigail Tuggle hadn't told Fargo her daughter had a mean streak. Was it an oversight on her part? Fargo doubted Jessie would prove to be Hilary. A banker's daughter, especially one who worked in the bank and met customers every day, would be a fine lady, not prone to fly off the handle. He said, "I'll make it a point to meet her. What's Jessie's last name?"

"Davis. She's riding in a Conestoga with a man named Jeek O'Grady. You'll know Jeek when you see him. Big handlebar mustache. A strong man, but sort of slow of mind."

Fargo's mind's eye reviewed the encounter with the feisty redhead who had bumped into the Ovaro. A fellow with a handlebar mustache and a belt pistol had appeared. Fargo grunted, "I think I've seen them. Did a bald-headed man show attention to them?"

"Not that I noticed. The only reason why I noticed Jessie and Jeek was because of one of my boys. Ralph Dirkson and Jeek got into a fight. I pulled them apart. Ralph told me Jessie paid him attention, you know, encouraged him. Ralph's a big man, like you, and a handsome devil."

Fargo concluded that if Jessie was Hilary, then she and John had not only taken on new names but were in different wagons as well. He wondered why. Fargo changed the subject. "Did a blond-haired man, kind of short and wiry, a friendly sort with an engaging smile, pass you folks in the last twenty-four hours?"

"Nobody has passed us. Coming or going."

Jude had answered all of Fargo's questions. Nothing more was said until the Trailsman was astride his pinto. Looking down at Jude, Fargo thanked him, then he nudged the stallion's flanks and rode away in the rain.

As he rode close to the Kansas River, Fargo's thoughts returned to John and Hilary. He sensed Hilary would turn out to be Jessie Davis. The bald-headed man drinking water from the barrel was her father. The more he thought about it, the more convinced he became. Fargo reasoned that they had plenty-enough money to buy and outfit two Conestogas and hire bodyguards to travel with them and do all the hard work. He would know soon enough. This same deluge would also stop Harley Skaggs dead in his tracks. Fargo slowed the Ovaro's gait to a walk.

Daylight faded to dark. He pressed on into the night. The hard rainfall slackened to a steady drizzle. About midnight, Fargo reined to a halt at a rush of weeping willows, dismounted, and went to work constructing a lean-to out of the willows. He stripped, then got inside his bedroll and lay there listening to the churning of the swollen river and the drizzle patter on top of the lean to. Within moments the monotonous sounds put him to sleep.

Dawn awakened him to see clear skies. Relieving himself, he decided against making a fire to brew coffee. The wet wood would be too time-consuming. Besides, the sooner he rode on, the sooner he would catch Skaggs. Walking from the riverbank to the lean-to, he saw the torrential rain had washed away all evidence that a wagon train had recently passed this way. He mounted up and continued to follow the Kansas River.

Belvue Village, then Wamego fell behind the Ovaro, without Skaggs' wagons being seen or any signs left by them. Two days later he was on the Big Blue, a tributary to the Kansas, and still he had not seen any evidence of Skaggs' wagons.

Well below Marysville the Little Blue branched into the Big Blue. Surely, Fargo mused to himself, Skaggs would stay on the California Trail and follow the Little Blue as far as it went to Ft. Kearney. He took the Little Blue. Within the hour he came to wheel ruts. Studying the tracks, he muttered, "Damn, the man must be whipping those oxen teams to run."

Two days went by. He still had not caught up with the wagons that had left the ruts, and they were freshly made, certainly no longer than by a day. Something was wrong, he concluded. Had he bypassed Skaggs altogether? Were these ruts made by the wagon train ahead of Skaggs? Had Skaggs left the California Trail? Surely the greenhorn had more sense than to do such a foolhardy thing, Fargo told himself. But it appeared he had done just that.

"The fool could be anywhere," Fargo muttered. "If not behind me, then left or right of the trail." Sighing heavily, he decided not to ride lengthy switchbacks to find the reckless man, but to continue straight for Ft. Kearney and wait for him there.

The wisdom of his reasoning was confirmed when he saw a long line of Conestogas parked in Belvedere, Nebraska, by the Little Blue. He doubted the wagon master would be Harley Skaggs, although he had to make sure.

Most of the settlers were on the ground. Fargo scanned their faces as he rode past. While he saw several who resembled Abigail's descriptions, for one reason or another they didn't match close enough to cause the big man to give pause. A distinct difference in clothing separated the settlers from the wagon master and his men. Fargo reined the Ovaro to a halt at the first weather-beaten man he came to.

"Where will I find the wagon master?" Fargo asked.

The man nodded toward the saloon. "Pete stepped inside to refresh himself."

Touching the brim of his hat, Fargo angled the Ovaro in the direction of the saloon. Inside, he found four men standing at the bar. Three were settlers. He asked the fourth, "Your name Pete?"

The man sized him up while nodding.

"My name is Fargo."

Pete nodded again.

"Back in Lawrence, Shorty Stubblefield and I had drinks. The saloon girl said there was a man looking to kill me. He's ahead of me by about a day. Blond hair. Short and wiry. Have you seen him?"

"Yep. Rode by yesterday shortly before dark. Seemed friendly enough, but later two of the women told me the fellow had winked at them. I don't put up with that kind of shit. Why does he want to kill you?"

"I beat him up back in St. Louis," Fargo answered, and let it go at that.

"Hunh," Pete snorted. "You should've killed the miserable little fucker."

"I know. I made a mistake. But I'll correct it when

and if we meet again. What kind of a horse was he on?"

"A dun mare about seventeen hands tall."

Fargo ordered a shot of bourbon, tossed it down, then left.

He followed days-old ruts the rest of the way to Ft. Kearney on the Platte River. He entered the town at sunset and started looking for the dun. Within a block on the main street he spotted four: one at the post office, another hitched to a post in front of the sheriff's office, and one standing in the middle of a long row of horses hitched to rails at the saloon. He missed seeing the fourth until it swished its tail. Fargo angled over to have a closer look. The saddled horse was tied to the banister of outside stairs that led up to the second story of the hotel. The saloon was right next to the hotel, separated by no more than eight feet. The dun mare could easily kick a hole in the saloon wall. Easing off his saddle, Fargo looked up the shadowy staircase. He tied the Ovaro next to the last horse at the rail in front of the saloon, in clear sight of anybody coming down the stairs. Then he went inside the hotel lobby.

A man with pork-chop sideburns greeted him cheerily. Rubbing his hands, the clerk smiled, then said, "Warm evening, isn't it, mister?"

Fargo nodded as he turned the open room journal around so he could read the names. He saw Chad Stark had gotten Room #8. "Is eight on the second floor?" he asked.

Miffed, the clerk spun the journal back like it had been. He snapped, "Yes, it is. But the room is assigned to another guest. I can put you in four, downstairs."

For an instant Fargo considered breaking down Chad's door and confronting him. But he decided against doing that. He wanted Chad Stark to come to him. Gunplay in a room where the door had been busted in would be hard for him to explain away. No, Fargo told himself, it's better that plenty of witnesses be present. Looking up the inside staircase, Fargo muttered, "Tell the man in Room Eight I will be waiting for him in the saloon."

The clerk gulped.

Grim-jawed, Fargo turned from the registration counter and ambled out the front door. He went to the saloon. As he often did, he paused outside the double doors to study those inside and spot potential trouble and its makers before entering. Fargo scanned the crowd in the noisy, smoke-filled room.

Troopers, mule-skinners, townsmen, wranglers, and frontiersmen stood two rows deep along the full length of the long bar. Others sat at poker tables. Spectators holding drinks stood around them. A boisterous crowd of men surrounded the crap table at the rear of the saloon. Several troopers were trying their luck at the wheel of fortune. A chorus line of slim to shapely to fleshy saloon girls mingled with the men.

Fargo watched a trooper rise from his chair at the poker table in the back corner. A raven-haired whore led him away.

The Trailsman pushed inside and headed for the trooper's vacated seat. He wanted it because the chair sat in the corner, a perfect position for seeing anybody coming into the room.

Fargo sat and bought a hundred dollars' worth of chips from the house dealer, who said, "This game is five-card stud. There ain't no jokers. Ante is one dollar. First high card up on my left bets."

"I know how to play the game," Fargo grunted. "Deal the cards."

After playing two hands, and losing both to a silver-haired man—Fargo reckoned he made his living gambling; the man dressed like a gambler and even smoked a slim cheroot—Fargo saw two familiar faces enter the saloon. They had tried in vain to change their personas. Levi's, boots, vests, and frontier hats couldn't take the city out of the crooked dice-players. One stood about two inches taller than the other. He was heavier, too. Fargo figured him to be a six-foot, two-hundred-pounder. He had dark-brown hair, bushy eyebrows above wide-set eyes, and was clean-shaven. Fargo guessed his age would be in the low thirties.

His blond partner was a few years younger and wore a trimmed beard and mustache. He smoked an average-sized curved-stem pipe.

The two headed straight to the crap table. Fargo kept one eye on them and the other on his cards. Whenever a person appeared at the entrance, he glanced up to see if it was Chad. The bastard would come in sooner or later.

The silver-haired man won again. Out of the corner of his eyes, Fargo saw the shorter of the crooked dice-handlers nudge his friend and nod toward Fargo's table. It was obvious the fellow had noticed Fargo. They moseyed over to the poker table and stood to watch Fargo play.

When the gambling man drew in yet another pot—Fargo reckoned he possessed an uncanny memory for keeping track of the cards—two wranglers announced they'd had enough and left the table. Fargo watched the two errant citifieds in sheep's clothing quickly take their seats.

While the dealer began shuffling, the blond looked at Fargo, smiled, then asked, "Didn't Brandon and I see you in a tub of hot water back in St. Louis?"

Fargo nodded.

Offering his hand to Fargo, the blond went on, "Name's Philo. Philo Markum."

Fargo shook hands with Philo, who had a firm grip. "Mine's Skye Fargo." He wondered why Philo and Brandon had shifted to five-card stud.

Sticking his hand out for Fargo to take, Brandon surprised the big man by saying, "We're private detectives from Chicago." Brandon grinned and added, "These damn clothes we're wearing are uncomfortable. I cannot get used to wearing a hat."

Brandon also had a firm handshake. Fargo probed, "I thought craps were you men's games?"

Philo chuckled. "Not out here," he explained.

Brandon added wryly, "We've found that they play craps for keeps west of the Mississippi."

The implication was clear enough for Fargo. He imagined them fleeing from a few crap tables before the threat of swinging on the end of a rope finally kept their crooked dice deep down in their pockets. The pair was friendly enough and had mended their ways, at least temporarily. And they hadn't hurt Fargo. Chicago kept rolling over in his mind.

He probed further, "What are you doing in Kearney?"

Philo answered, "On assignment. We are looking for a man and his daughter. They are believed to have stolen a lot of money."

Abigail Tuggle hadn't mentioned hiring two private detectives, Fargo thought. He had to be sure. He waited until the next hand was over—the silver-haired gambler won with a queen high showing, then turned his hole card over, another queen—before inquiring, "What do they look like, this man and his daughter? I might run across them."

Brandon gave him John and Hilary's descriptions, then offered, "We have reason to believe they are on a wagon train going to San Francisco."

Philo interrupted to admit, "We got lost immediately after that, uh, unfortunate misunderstanding, shall we say, back in St. Louis. We've been wandering around with our thumbs stuck up in our asses ever since. And we're still lost. We may never find them . . . and the money."

Brandon, the more observant of the two detectives, had apparently kept his eyes on the cards while talking to Fargo and Philo. Three cards had been dealt to each player. The gambling man had a pair of deuces showing. Fargo had noticed he customarily left his hole card lying on the table when he peeked at it. Other times he would pick it up with both hands. This was one of those times. After studying his hole card briefly, Silver-Hair removed his right hand and lowered it palm-down on top of the table, then with his left hand slipped the card facedown beneath the edge of one deuce. Brandon had obviously noticed Silver-Hair's departure from custom. The man sitting on Silver-Hair's right had opened with a jack. Now he deferred to the pair of deuces.

When Silver-Hair shoved ten dollars out, Brandon spoke. "Friend, I think you got into the discards. Raise your right hand kind of slow like."

All eyes cut to Silver-Hair's right hand. He slowly drew it toward him. Four revolvers appeared over the edge of the table and pointed at his chest. Silver-Hair started stammering, "Well, er, uh, ah, I must say, er, uh, I've never—"

"Hold it right there, friend," Brandon hissed. His left hand shot to and covered Silver-Hair's right. Using the index finger on his right hand, Brandon flipped over the hole card. Everybody saw a third deuce. Then Brandon turned Silver-Hair's right hand palm-up. Everybody saw a ten in it.

It takes a thief to catch a thief, Fargo thought. Brandon had caught Silver-Hair palming cards. Their value made no difference; sooner or later the palmed card would make a hand.

The only thing that saved Silver-Hair from getting a one-way ticket to the hanging tree was Chad Stark's appearance at the swinging doors, and Fargo's announcement, "Get away from this table, men. There's going to be a killing."

They followed his stare to Chad, who was returning Fargo's icy stare. Chairs scooted back. The players quickly rose and stepped out of the line of fire. One echoed Fargo's warning in a loud voice, "There's going to be a shoot-out. Everyone get back and give 'em room."

All conversations ceased abruptly. The wheel of fortune clacked to a halt. Then the rush was on. Those closest to the double doors darted through them. Others fled out the back door. Several ran up the stairs. Chad Stark walked measuredly to the center of the bar. Those standing at it divided and gave the two men plenty of room.

Chad halted and half-turned. Without taking his eyes off Fargo's, he shouted, "That man is a thief.

Earlier he robbed me at gunpoint and took ten ten-dollar bills, all I had on me."

Fargo rose slowly and planted both hands flat on the tabletop. He growled, "That's a lie."

Stark spun and fired. The screaming slug nicked the upper arm of Fargo's gun hand. As he drew and fired his Colt, Fargo heard the bullet chew into the wall behind him. Fargo's shot went high and to the right. It grazed Chad's right shoulder. His revolver clattered on the wooden floor. Before Fargo could squeeze off a killing round, a trooper's hand knocked the Colt from his gun hand. Two husky troopers pinned Fargo to the back wall.

Chad suggested they check Fargo for the ten bills. Brandon emptied Fargo's pockets and spread the money on the tabletop so everybody could see. There weren't any ten-dollar bills. Chad said, "Check his horse. He rides that big black-and-white pinto hitched outside."

Two men hurried through the double doors to go and check. While they were gone, Philo said in a reassuring tone, "They won't find anything. I know you're innocent, Fargo. I'm sure of it."

But Fargo wasn't so sure, and the two men proved it when they returned. One waved the ten bills as he cried, "Just like he said! We found the money in that one's saddlebags. He's guilty, all right."

An older, rotund man dressed in a black business suit stepped into the center of the room, looked at Fargo, and said, "Most of you boys know me. Those who do not, I'm telling you I'm Dudley Albright, the circuit judge in these parts, better known as the Hanging Judge. Now, all of you heard and saw everything same as me. So I'm making you all the jury. I'll entertain a voice vote of guilty or not guilty on the man pinned to the wall before pronouncing sentence."

A few not-guilties were drowned out in the loud chorus of guilties.

Judge Albright rubbed his chin as he obviously thought about Fargo's fate. Finally the judge spoke. "You have been found guilty by your peers, good and honest men all. Now, ordinarily, theft is a hanging offense. But because nobody actually saw you rob the plaintiff, but found his money in your saddlebags, I'm forced to go on circumstantial evidence. So I'm sentencing you to six months in jail." Pointing to a man, he told him, "Go get Sheriff Oliver Eggleston."

Chad Stark smiled victoriously.

9

Stripped to the waist, Skye Fargo lay on his army cot in Sheriff Eggleston's jail and stared thoughtfully at the ceiling. A heavy film of perspiration covered his body. Not a breath of air circulated in the jail or the adjacent office, where the sheriff sat at his small desk. Deputy Frank Albright, a nephew of the circuit judge, stood in the open doorway. He fanned his face with his hat. The only sounds were made by a pair of horse-flies buzzing in Fargo's cell. The flies had been there since Eggleston locked him up two and half days ago.

Fargo was thinking about how he could escape. He had to break out. If he languished in jail for the full six months, John and Hilary would be hopelessly lost to him somewhere on the West Coast. He could find Horatio Arnold easily enough, but the possibility always existed that John wouldn't contact him, or if he did, what was to say Horatio would know of his present whereabouts. After six months the trail would be ice-cold.

His left hand moved unconsciously to the inch-long scab on his upper right arm. When he glanced to the ribbon wound, his thoughts turned to Chad Stark. The wily little man had gulled him, and had done a good job at it. Stark had taken the precaution of hiding the ten bills in Fargo's saddlebags. If he didn't gun me down, Fargo thought for the umpteenth time, he could fall back on my saddlebags.

Fargo propped up on an elbow and looked through the bars at his gun belt, which was hanging on a peg in the front wall of the office. His Colt rode in its holster, so close and yet so far away. His Sharps stood in the rack at the same wall. Sheriff Eggleston had put his Arkansas toothpick and its calf sheath in the lower right-hand drawer of his desk. Fargo felt naked without his weapons.

One of the green flies broke his fixation on his gun belt. He blinked, then lay back down and looked at the ten-foot-high ceiling again. After the sheriff had locked him up and gone home that first night, Fargo had stood on the cot and tested the ceiling's strength. No amount of pushing could budge any of the boards. A narrow, horizontal-barred, and open window was mounted dead-center where the ceiling joined the rear wall of the jail. He'd tried the bars also and found none loose. Then he'd tested the three walls, then each of the cell's bars. Eggleston's jail seemed impregnable insofar as escape was concerned. Still, the big man thought about it. He reminded himself he'd thought his way out of worse situations than he was in now, and if he continued to think, he would discover the flaw in this one.

He glanced up at the barred window. The angle of the sun indicated the hour to be about four o'clock. The bright rays coming through the opening painted a stark contrasting black-and-white pattern on the wooden floor.

Fargo closed his lake-blue eyes to nap. Several heartbeats later he heard a low rumble and the babble of loud voices. He sat up, opened his eyes, and listened more closely. A wagon train was entering Ft. Kearney. He moved to the bars to watch the passage. Was it Jude Crowley's voice he heard, or Harley Skaggs'?

"Wagon train coming, Sheriff," Frank said, and put his hat on.

Eggleston pushed back from his desk. He and Frank stepped outside to watch. Fargo saw the mule-skinner-turned-wagon-master Harley Skaggs and his two young helpers come into view, then the lead wagons.

Skaggs barked, "Whoa! Stop 'em, boys. Let 'em rest for thirty minutes."

The next wagon halted directly in front of the sheriff's office and jail. Fargo saw Jeek O'Grady holding the whip. Sitting beside him was the redheaded spitfire Fargo had tangled with earlier, before he visited Abigail Tuggle. He knew at once the redhead was Hilary. As he watched, Jeek helped her down from the Conestoga's seat. Hilary stretched, then walked out of Fargo's sight. Jeek headed toward the saloon.

Fifteen long minutes passed before she reappeared. This time John was with her, and his "companion," Barney Ruttman.

Ruttman watered the oxen while John and Hilary stood talking. Five more minutes went by, then Jeek, the two detectives, and Chad Stark joined them.

Fargo put his wild-creature hearing to work. Straining to eavesdrop their conversation, he picked out of it enough words to let him know more.

Jeek said, "I met these here men over in the saloon." He went on to introduce the trio. Only thing wrong was, they had changed their names. Fargo heard Jeek call Chad Mr. Orville Gunnison; Philo, Mr. Kurt Hoffmeister; and Brandon, Mr. George Taylor. They talked about joining the wagon train. John said they would have to see if it was all right with the wagon master. Jeek said he would be glad to fix their meals.

Hilary said, "Like hell! Only if they provide the fixings." She seemed especially cold toward Chad and kept edging farther and farther away from him.

Skaggs stalked past the group. Jeek flagged him down and introduced him to the newcomers. They asked if they could join the wagon train. Harley made a show of it, shifting his weight twice while rubbing his jaw, as though giving the request serious consideration but having reservations. Fargo knew what the mule-skinner was doing. Harley was jacking up the price. Finally, he cited an amount for each. They shook hands. Money changed hands. Harley walked away. The detectives, Chad, and Jeek headed for the saloon.

John and Hilary watched them go. Fargo heard her wonder aloud, "Do you think they know?"

Her father shrugged, then he, too, moved out of Fargo's sight. Hilary turned and looked toward the sheriff's office. Shielding her eyes against the bright sunlight, she stared directly at Fargo, took a pace forward, paused, then turned and went behind her wagon.

Fargo heard Jeek yell, "Barney, get over here, quick!"

The Trailsman watched Barney saunter toward the saloon. Fargo then muttered the answer to Hilary's wonderment, "Yes, Hilary, they know about the money. All of them know."

Fargo had questions of his own. Like, how did Barney and Jeek fit into the scheme of things? Where was the money? Jeek was sluggish, yes, but not Ruttman. Surely Ruttman knew where the money was stashed. Why was he waiting for Jeek and him to make off with it? The only answer the big man staring through the bars would think of was, Ruttman planned to steal the stolen money in California. Would he have Jeek kill John and Hilary if necessary? That answer was simple enough: Yes!

Fargo stood at the bars a moment longer, then returned to his smelly cot and reclined. The flies buzzed in front of his face. His gun hand shot out and snatched one. Fargo briefly considered squashing the little nuisance trapped in his fist, decided against it, and opened his hand. The fly just sat there on his palm. Fargo had to shoo it away.

Moments later he heard Harley Skaggs' whiny voice order the settlers, "All right! Everybody take your seats. This here wagon train is moving out. Lucky, you and Goose see to it that there ain't no stragglers. Yoh! Roll 'em!"

Fargo moved to the bars to watch the wagons leave. Counting the two he'd seen before Harley halted them, he counted seven more, all Conestogas. Chad rode alongside Hilary's wagon, Philo and Brandon next to John's. Now that they had found the culprits, they were sticking close to the money like a glob of glue. Fargo chuckled at the absurdity of it all.

Four lonely days went by before Fargo heard the next wagon train rumble into Ft. Kearney. Fargo stepped to the bars in time to glimpse Jude Crowley ride past the sheriff's office. He asked Deputy Albright to bring the wagon master to him.

Albright refused, saying, "I just know you're itching to bust out. You've been nervous as a cougar ever since we put you in that cell. Asking me to fetch a friend of yours might be doing something foolish on my part." He stepped outside before Fargo could make a rebuttal.

Six days later when Shorty Stubblefield and his crew and wagons came to town at sunset, Fargo didn't bother with being denied a second time. He bit his tongue and watched Shorty come and go. He watched other wagon trains come and go also. While Stubblefield's wagons were still in town, Fargo had called Sheriff Eggleston to the bars and sounded a warning. "Eggleston, you need to remind Shorty and all wagon masters following in his wake that there is a crazy Cheyenne medicine man on the loose near South Pass. Or, if you'd like, I'll tell him."

The sheriff had answered, "Fargo, I don't want anyone visiting you. I'll tell him myself."

After that Fargo left it up to the sheriff to warn the wagon masters taking the California Trail.

Fargo had been in jail three weeks and two days. He lay on his cot going over the daily routine. The last thing the sheriff did before going home for the night was to personally inspect the inside of Fargo's cell for security. The deputy stood outside and watched. After satisfying himself that all was indeed secure and that Fargo hadn't tampered with any boards or bars, Eggleston stepped out of the cell and watched while Frank locked it. When the two lawmen left, the front door was closed and locked, effectively sealing their prisoner inside. Fargo drifted off to sleep thinking how their safety precaution routine never varied.

During the early-morning hours, Fargo's wild-creature hearing picked up a soft sound inside the darkened cell. Instantly, Fargo's eyes popped open. His gun hand automatically slipped under his pillow and felt for his Colt. Long-standing habits were hard to break. Slowly, naturally for a sleeping man, he rolled over and looked for the source of the sound.

The frayed end of a strong rope snaked through the bars in the window and dangled invitingly. Fargo knew what to do. He rolled off the cot and pulled on his boots and shirt, then stepped to the rope. Moving swiftly, he tied it around two bars, then stepped back and waited.

He heard somebody slap a horse on the rump. A split second later, the bars and entire window broke free and crashed onto the ground. Fargo pressed up into the opening and looked out.

His saddled and otherwise trail-ready stallion stood at the other end of the rope, an Indian pony nearby. Imogene Talbot, dressed in the buckskin dress, smiled up at him and said, "What are you waiting for? Let's go."

Fargo crawled through the opening and dropped to the ground. Glancing to the Big Dipper, he saw it sat in the two-o'clock position. He said, "Wait here while I get my guns."

"Aw, Fargo, aren't you going to kiss me?"

"Not now, Imogene. Later, when we're on the trail." He went around the building, hugging the wall going to the front. Lamps still burned in the saloon across the wide street. Piano music spilled over the swinging doors. Fargo looked at the grimy window in front of the sheriff's office. He decided the loud music would mask the sound of it breaking. He stepped to the window and used his fist to break the glass in the lower right-hand corner. Holding his breath, he tapped out enough of the shattered pane to permit reaching in and unlocking the window. He raised it, crawled inside, and collected his weapons.

When he returned to the horses, Imogene was already astride her pony. She asked, "Aren't you going to ask how I found you?"

"No," he grunted, although he was a tad curious. "Later, when—"

"I know, I know," she interrupted. "When we're on the trail." Disgustedly, Imogene added, "You men! Later, later, later. That's all you know."

It felt good to be in the saddle again. He dug his heels into the Ovaro's flanks. They rode out of Ft. Kearney at a gallop, headed west, and followed the north bank of the Platte. Moments later the lamplight from the saloon became a tiny yellow, diffused blur. About ten miles from Kearney, Fargo reined to a halt next to where a stretch in the river ran shallow. He dismounted and immediately started pulling off his clothes.

Sliding off her pony, Imogene asked excitedly, "We're going to do it?"

"Not now," he said. "After you scrub this jail-house stink from my body."

"Oh, goody," she cooed. "I've never scrubbed a man before. This is going to be fun." She wiggled out of the buckskin dress and beat Fargo into the water by four strides.

Fargo lay on the sandy bottom and relished the cold water flowing over his body. "God, but I feel great," he said.

Imogene crawled to him. Scooping sand in her hands, she said, "Tell me if I'm too rough on you."

"Scrub hard," Fargo replied, and stretched his arms and legs wide.

Imogene made token passes on his chest and arms, but when she got to his muscular thighs, she let the grit slip through her fingers and grabbed his member. He pulled her atop him and accommodated the little filly.

Afterward they crawled to the grassy bank and lay there while their breaths and pounding hearts returned to normal.

Looking up at the star-filled sky, Fargo asked, "So how did you find me?"

"Fargo, you have to stop sleeping with whores. Really."

"What's that supposed to mean? I asked how you found me."

"After you, I knew it wouldn't work out for me in Chicago. Father told me you had gone to see Abigail Tuggle. So I paid her a visit. She told me everything. That woman has a weight problem. Huffs and puffs all the time. Keeps that fan moving, too."

She was rambling. Fargo prodded, "Imogene?"

"Well, anyhow, I rode straight for St. Louis. I knew you had visited the saloon across the street from our hotel. See? I remembered."

"Uh huh. Go on."

"Well, you should have seen the surprised looks on those men's faces when I walked into that saloon. Inez Swartz took me to her upstairs room where we had a little woman-to-woman talk. She told—"

"Whoa," Fargo blurted. "Inez Swartz?"

"Yeah, one of the women working in the saloon."

Fargo reckoned Inez was Dulce Doll. He said, "Continue."

"Inez told me she took you to the saloon owner and you all talked about the California Trail. So I met Mr. Keefer. He gave me a map showing the trail. I followed it." She paused and poked his shoulder, then said, "You didn't actually screw that skinny girl, Wanda Sue, did you?"

Amazing, Fargo thought, how females knew exactly how to hook up with one another. "What did Wanda Sue tell you?"

"I asked if she had seen a big man riding a big black-and-white stallion lately. She scratched her butt and said, 'Shit yeah, I seed him all right. Me an' Fargo, we fucked till the dadburned barn caved in all 'round us, and Pa shot the rooster deader'n a door-nail. Fargo, tell me you didn't do that."

He chuckled at the way Wanda Sue had exaggerated things a mite. His hand eased down and felt his poker when he remembered how sore it was when he rode away from Wanda Sue and her bony Venus mound.

"What's so funny?" Imogene asked, and poked his shoulder again.

"Nothing. Please continue."

"I stopped at every saloon I came to and asked the saloon girls if they had seen you and your horse. None had until I got to Topeka. One said you and Shorty Stubblefield came in for a drink. She said a man was looking for you, too. He said he was out to kill you. Now, why would he want to do that? I asked myself."

"Didn't Dulce Doll tell you?"

"Who's Dulce Doll?" Imogene answered, frowning, "I must have missed one."

"I meant to say Inez Swartz. She watched Chad and I fight."

"Who's Chad?"

"The man looking for me."

"Well, anyhow, I got my map and spread it on the bar. The saloon girl and bartender in Topeka showed me a shortcut to Fort Kearney."

And that explains how she got here so fast, Fargo thought.

Imogene continued, "I got to Kearney after dark last night. Boy howdy, that's a rough crowd back in that saloon. My butt got pinched black and blue by those army troopers. A saloon girl pulled me aside and gave me a piece of her mind about horning in on the customers. I told her I was—"

"Looking for a big man riding a big black-and-white stallion," Fargo interrupted.

"Uh huh. She said that made a difference, then told me all about you and that man—Chad?—having a gunfight and you going to jail. I thanked her, then went looking for your horse. I found him over in the livery. You know the rest. Did you find Mrs. Tuggle's husband and daughter?"

"Saw both, but didn't speak with them. I was behind bars at the time."

Gradually they fell asleep, still in each other's arms.

They awakened entwined at dawn, dressed, and rode west, sleeping under the stars at night until arriving at Scottsbluff, Nebraska Territory, near the Wyoming Territory border. There they shared a hotel room. Fargo didn't go to the saloon that night. They were up at first light, ate in a small café, then bought provisions for a few days. Fargo would have to shoot game to see them through until they caught up with Harley Skaggs' wagons.

They left Scottsbluff when the sun was half up on the horizon. It promised to be a pretty day, mildly warm and sunny. Not a cloud was in the sky.

At noon, Fargo left the meandering California Trail, which always followed close to water, crossed the North Platte just inside Wyoming, and headed straight west for South Pass. He hoped he could get there in time. The mule-skinner and his greenhorn youngsters would need all the help they could get should Kills Fast strike.

After riding about a mile they topped a low rise and saw the remains of three Conestogas in the meadow between it and the next rise, grim reminders that it was best to stay on the trail. They rode to the charred Conestogas. The canvas tops had been the first to go up in flames. All that remained were the steel supporting bands.

Fargo dismounted and started searching for any water that might remain. The wagons had been picked clean. What the other wagoneers didn't take, the Indians had. He found a Lakota arrow embedded in one side of a Conestoga.

Imogene called to him, "Over here, Fargo."

He went to her and saw she had found four graves. Prairie grass had grown over them. Fargo probed a finger into the mound of soil on one. He reckoned it had been spaded about two weeks earlier. Three of the graves were adult-length, the fourth covered a child no more than six years old. Boards removed from the wagons served as markers. The child's read: LENORA BLASINGAME, BORN AUG. 10, 1854, DIED FROM A RED SAVAGE'S ARROW AUG. 8, 1860. R.I.P. None of the adults was John or Hilary, or if they were, they had gone down together, without telling anyone their real names.

They mounted up and rode over the next rise. They saw no more wagons, only gorgeous landscape laced with an abundance of rippling streams. They crossed through and over the Laramie Mountain Range—a spectacular sight—then the Shirleys. They made camp on the Medicine Bow River after leaving the Shirley Mountains.

Fargo shot and dressed a six-point white-tail buck. They gorged themselves with venison that night. Two days later Fargo bagged a bighorn in the Green Mountains, the foothills of the Rockies. They were two days short of South Pass, the moment of truth. Skaggs should be there by then. If he wasn't, Fargo told himself, he would wait for one day, then backtrack on the California Trail to find out what had happened.

They rose with the sun and pressed on. The Antelope Hills slipped behind them, then at high noon the next day, South Pass loomed dead ahead. Black smoke rose from the pass, caught a high current of wind, and bent abruptly to send a stream of wispy smoke in it. Fargo feared the worst.

He sent the Ovaro up the side of the mountain at a dead run, yelling to Imogene, "Follow in my tracks as fast as you can. See you at the top."

Grimly, she nodded.

Fargo counted nine Conestogas on South Pass, four burning furiously. Bodies littered the ground. Settlers were using their priceless water in an attempt to save two of the burning wagons. The other two were too far gone for any amount of water. The people seemed confused. Crying women clutched their little ones to them. Men not fighting the fires stood perplexed. Cheyenne arrows protruded from the dead. Fargo dismounted and asked one of the bystanders where he could find the wagon master. He expected to hear, "Chasing down those red savages."

Instead, the man stammered, "Skaggs, he, he and one of his men, they, they left us to, to fend for ourselves. They're gone. Down that way." He pointed through the pass. "The other got killed. The bastard left us. The savages—a short, mean-looking man wearing a bear-claw necklace—he, he took Miss Jessie Davis."

"Is Jessie redheaded?" Fargo wanted to know.

Before the man could answer, Imogene rode up and dismounted.

Fargo told her, "This is the wagon train the Tuggles are on. Start looking for them. Don't talk to them, though. Kills Fast took a female captive. I'll try to save her." He climbed into the saddle. Looking down at the man, he repeated, "Does Jessie have red hair?"

The befuddled man nodded. "I think so."

"Which way did the Indians go?"

The man pointed in the direction in which Fargo had arrived, and that told him Chief Many Horses had not yet broken camp and moved. Fargo wheeled the Ovaro and dug his boot heels into his flanks. The stallion must have sensed a forthcoming battle. Snorting, he squatted, reared, and came down charging hard.

Fargo hadn't seen the Cheyenne war party coming down the mountain. That meant they had either reached the bottom or angled off into the dense mountain forest. He hoped it would prove to be the latter, for he took to the forest.

As he rode among the tall pine, he watched for signs of ponies in the dappled sunlight bursting through the green canopy. He saw no signs. Fargo smelled and saw evidence of *tiospaye* tepees from a mile away. Smoke wafting from the many cooking fires clung to the ground much like a thin, patchy fog. The closer he got to the encampment, the more pronounced the white smoke became.

Fargo reined the Ovaro to a halt in a swath of golden aspen above the tepees. He dismounted and withdrew the Sharps from its saddle case, then moved to and crouched at the edge of the tree line. He saw many braves wearing war paint and heard their war cries. They were in a jovial, victorious mood, strutting about, laughing, slapping one another on the back. Two held scalps high. Others spread bolts of material on the ground in the open area where Fargo had been dragged. The medicine man emerged out of his tepee and shouted a command. All activity ceased. The people became attentive.

Fargo heard Kills Fast call for a victory dance. "Many white-eyes died this day," he began. "Their wagons burn as I speak. The spirits have been good to us, my warriors. We will honor the spirits with a dance. *Hoka!*"

Women immediately brought wood to the fire burning in the center of the circle. Fargo watched two warriors carry a large war drum to the south perimeter of the area and set it down. Six other warriors armed with drumsticks started beating the drum. Women huddled around them and picked up on the fast beat and began their high-pitched chanting. The warriors stomped the ground as they danced around the fire. Fargo didn't see Many Horses or his wives.

He reckoned they were away. In the absence of Many Horses, the cruel medicine man had seized the opportunity to attack the wagon train unhindered. Fargo sat to watch the Cheyenne dance and to wait for night to fall.

The victory dance lasted well into the night. Ominous, dark clouds roiled over the mountaintops, moving from west to east. The temperature dropped dramatically. The deathly still air carried moisture. Not a leaf on the aspens quavered. It was going to rain. Fargo donned his poncho, then returned to sit and watch and wait.

Finally the drum fell silent. Women led the exhausted warriors to tepees. Within moments the encampment appeared deserted. The silence hung heavy. Then Fargo heard a female scream. He knew to move his studious gaze onto the medicine man's tepee. Hilary Tuggle was indeed alive, albeit suffering a horrible ordeal.

"Well," he muttered, "she is paying a penalty for what she and her father did back in Chicago."

From the light cast by the dwindling fire Fargo saw the door flap to Chief Many Horses' tepee be opened. First, One Feather, then Pretty Grass stepped through the opening. They looked toward Kills Fast's tepee on the far side of the open space, then conversed in hushed voices so quiet that Fargo's wild-creature hearing couldn't discern what they said. They turned and went back inside the tepee.

Fargo moved down to stand behind a large pine. He threw a pebble and hit the covering on Many Horses' tepee, then waited for one of the wives to come investigate. When neither did, he tossed two more pebbles in rapid succession. This time Pretty Grass came outside and went to the place where the pebbles had hit. Fargo pitched another one to draw her attention to him. After picking up the pebble and examining it, she looked in the direction from where it was thrown. Fargo stepped into the clear and waved to Pretty Grass. He knew she could see him in the fire's glow.

She spotted him. He signed for her and One Feather to come to the aspen grove. Pretty Grass went inside the tepee. Fargo moved back to the aspen. Shortly, the two women met him.

Fargo asked, "Where is Many Horses?"

They lowered their eyes. One Feather answered, "Many Horses has gone to the spirit world, across the great waters in the south, to join his relatives."

Pretty Grass explained, "He perished in the sweat lodge when you were in it. He helped us hold down Kills Fast long enough for you to escape. But Kills Fast was too strong for us to hold. He shoved our husband onto the stone people. I can still hear his flesh frying."

One Feather recounted what had happened next. "Kills Fast pulled us out of the lodge. He beat us hard for what we did. Then he threw us back inside and ordered his warriors to close the door and not open it again until the stone people died. Trailsman, it was hot in there. Did you come for the white woman Kills Fast captured?"

"Yes, and I need your help."

"Anything, Trailsman," Pretty Grass replied. "Kill the man and put an end to his torment. He's crazy in the head."

"I won't take his life if I can keep from doing it. That will be his decision. But I will punish him severely. Here's what I want you to do. Go call the medicine man outside. Tell him I am watching. Say I will meet him at the fire only when I see no warriors anywhere around. Tell him that. Say he is to give up the white woman. Only then will I leave peaceably. Tell him I won't fight him unless he forces me to. Think you can remember all I said?"

Both women nodded.

"Then go." He watched them turn and leave.

Pretty Grass rapped on Kills Fast's tepee door flap. The medicine man's head poked through the opening. The women obviously repeated Fargo's instructions, for he saw the medicine man burst out of the opening and look to find him. When Kills Fast cupped a hand to his mouth, clearly an indication that he intended to call out his warriors, Pretty Grass yanked the hand away. Clear as a bell, Fargo heard her repeat his warning, "The Trailsman will come to the fire only when he sees no warriors anywhere around."

With his eyes searching the darkened forest, Kills Fast strutted about with his chest thrown out. Finally he nodded and went inside his tepee. One Feather signed that it was safe for Fargo to come on down. Fargo led the Ovaro down into the circle.

Kills Fast shoved Hilary through the opening. She was naked, of course. Then he dragged her, stumbling, next to the fire and forced her onto her knees. Fargo used her assumed name when asking, "Jessie, are you all right?"

"Yeah, I guess I'm okay," she spat. "If you call taking a beating then a raping all right." She brushed her red hair back and stared venomously at the medicine man.

Kills Fast looked at Fargo and said, "I intend to kill you, then the woman, white man. I want you out of my life. She's no good. Her hole is too big." He drew his scalping knife and fell into a crouch.

Four lightning bolts ripped from the clouds and exploded as many trees. The spirits in the west were watching this fight. Then a torrential downpour fell. Fargo drew his Arkansas toothpick and startled circling with Kills Fast, searching for an opening that would let him kill the tough little medicine man. Hilary was trapped in the middle of their circling. She alternately watched Fargo then Kills Fast. Pretty Grass and One Feather stood clear of the two men, waiting for the outcome. The fire sputtered in rebellion of the rain.

Thunder boomed and rumbled down the mountainside. Kills Fast leapt over his naked captive and lunged the scalping knife at Fargo's throat. The big man dodged in time to prevent the knife from cutting his throat. Kills Fast's blade cut into Fargo's left upper arm.

Fargo parried with Kills Fast. He nimbly pitched the stiletto from hand to hand as he went around the medicine man in increasingly smaller circles. He saw that Kills Fast took his eyes off the flashing blade from time to time to see where he was in relation to Hilary. Fargo edged him closer and closer to her. He figured she would trip Kills Fast, but the man stumbled over her instead.

Quick as a wink, Fargo yanked him to his feet. Both men's blades pressed against each other's throat. The medicine man blinked. Fargo slashed. Kills Fast dropped like a falling rock onto the fire's glowing embers. His flesh sizzled. Fargo wiped his blade clean on the dead man's loincloth. He looked at Pretty Grass and One Feather. They had turned and were walking through the mud, heading for their tepee.

Pulling Hilary upright, Fargo said, "Let's get out of here, Jessie."

10

The night storm raged in full fury, sending torrents of rainwater cascading down the mountainside through the forest and into the valley below. Even the mighty pinto stallion was having trouble keeping his footing, which created a far more life-threatening situation for Hilary Tuggle than her horrendous experience with the maniacal Cheyenne medicine man. Nonetheless, it was absolutely nothing to the naked female firebrand. She bitched, she complained bitterly, she cursed, she yelled and screamed, she wailed and gnashed her teeth, and she fell off the horse.

For an instant Fargo considered leaving her lying in the downward-rushing muddy water. It took a monstrous bolt of lightning that peeled all the bark off a stately Douglas fir nearby to change his mind. The brilliance of the blast lasted an extremely long time. During the radiant ozone-producing explosion, Fargo saw the woman down on all fours, struggling against the forces seeking to overpower her. Muddy water crashed against her naked body much like angry seawater crashing over a rocky stretch of beach. She was totally helpless against the onslaught and was about to be swept down the mountainside. He felt pity for her.

"Help me," she cried. "Oh, God, help me!"

Fargo was already out of the saddle and groping to find her. The current had caught and moved the woman from where he saw her during the illumination. "Keep shouting," he yelled.

When she screamed, he moved toward her voice. She was farther away than he imagined. Blindly, he waved his hands low over the churning, muddy water. His gun hand met flesh where her thighs changed into buttocks. Hilary didn't protest. She grabbed his left arm and pulled. He shoved his hand through her thighs and lifted her out of the rain-swollen mud. She clutched his shoulders and buried her face in his powerful chest. With his arm still between her thighs and his hand gripping her buttock cheeks, he carried her to the Ovaro. Lightning flashed. The stallion's jet-black fore- and hind-quarters and pure-white midsection fairly glistened in the rain.

Fargo put her fanny next to the pommel of his saddle so she could ride facing him, then he mounted up. He suggested, "Lean on my chest and hold on. We're not out of the woods yet." When she did, he dropped the front of his poncho over her. He nudged the Ovaro to proceed at a slow walk.

Hilary curled an arm around Fargo's neck and pressed her chest to his. The cold rain, he discovered, had brought her nipples fully erect and made the twin peaks rock-hard. Even through his shirt he felt them stabbing his pectoral muscles. He willed his organ to not be aroused. Not here, he thought, not now.

Slowly the Ovaro threaded his way through the rain-drenched mountain forest to the trail that led up to the pass. Unhindered by trees, rocks, and dense undergrowth, the rainwater ran free on the open trail. The cleared path had been visited by so many runoffs before that the topsoil had been carried into the valley below. The Ovaro made faster progress.

Thunder roared across the mountain and reverberated off others in the distance. Lightning ripped through the ugly clouds. The heavenly display lit up the Conestogas parked on South Pass. Fargo saw nobody outside their wagons. The dead had been removed. He asked Hilary, "Which wagon is yours?"

She twisted to look. Pointing to the lead wagon, she said, "That one. Where is everybody?"

He dared a chuckle. "Why, inside, out of the rain, of course." He came alongside her Conestoga and helped her onto the driver's seat. A babble of male voices came from within the dark interior of the wagon.

Hilary asked, "Aren't you coming in out of the rain?"

Fargo shook his head. Jeek O'Grady poked his head through the tightly drawn front opening of the canvas top. His widened eyes looked at Hilary, then at the big black-and-white and the man sitting easy in the saddle. Fargo touched the brim of his wet hat, and said, "I'll be back at daybreak." He encouraged the stallion into a walk and continued riding on through South Pass.

The wagons and oxen teams, shrouded in the heavy downpour, faded from his view. He rode eight miles before angling left and leaving the trail near a large outcrop of jagged rocks. Hidden by thickets gaped the narrow opening of a cave he knew was there. Fargo dismounted and led the Ovaro through the tight mouth of the cave. He fumbled in his saddlebags to find his matches. He struck one and looked around the huge cavern. Dry firewood left by Indians seeking shelter during storms like this one lay on the equally dry floor. All it took was one more match for flames to erupt on the piece of pitch pine nestled among fast-burning, split yellow pine. Fargo had a warm fire going in short order. He took his saddle and other stuff off the Ovaro. After letting his stallion drink from the canteen, the horse moseyed to the back of the cave and lay down. Fargo set the coffeepot to brewing, then spread his bedroll and lay on it while waiting for the coffee to boil.

His thoughts returned to his earlier wonderment regarding what John and Hilary had done with the stolen money. Surely they had it in one of the wagons; otherwise, why bother with the hardships of the wagon train going to San Francisco if the money was left somewhere back East? Fargo tried to imagine the size of the stack of bills. He couldn't. The mix of denominations would determine the bulk. That and the dollar amount. Abigail didn't know, or if she did, she hadn't said. Fargo reasoned the denominations were such as to produce a minimal stack, probably in a size that could be carried in a large handbag.

Jeek and Barney knew about the money. They had to know. How they learned about it was inconsequential. And they had obviously told the detectives and Chad Stark. Were the detectives and Chad among the dead after the Cheyenne attack? He would know in the morning. Was John? Had his wagon burned? With the money? The questions had to wait for dawn to be answered.

The lid on the coffeepot rattled and broke his train of thought. He filled his tin cup with the hot brew. Sipping, he picked up on his thoughts. The fact that Jeek had brought Philo, Brandon, and Chad into the scheme of things clearly suggested a great amount of money, enough for all five to share. Bringing them in also suggested Jeek and Barney had not found the money; otherwise, it was stupid of them to tell the trio.

Fargo's thought drifted to Hilary. Her lower lips had kissed his forearm when he shoved his hand between her thighs. She had a nice ass, too. Firm, rounded. She weighed about 120 pounds sopping wet. Her breasts were quite full and firm. Fargo recalled glimpsing them as she knelt beside the fire in the circle of death. Hilary could be a most desirable female, he decided. If only she wasn't so damn testy.

He quit thinking, downed his coffee, then undressed and got inside his bedroll. Fargo was asleep within seconds.

The stallion moving about at the rear of the cave awakened him. He looked through the opening. Dawn was breaking in clear skies. Enough embers remained in the fire to reheat his coffeepot. He pushed it down into the hot coals, then went outside to take a leak. Rainwater still trickled down the brushy slope. He added his stream to the flow. A gaggle of crows flew low from behind him, caw-cawed as they picked up speed, and headed toward the wagons.

Fargo stretched, then went back inside to have his morning coffee. Minutes later he had the Ovaro made ready for the trail and led him outside. He walked the horse to the trail, mounted up, and rode to the wagons, hoping to learn some of the answers to last night's questions. He decided to go along with all their assumed names while sorting out things.

He saw they had split logs to get at the dry inner cores to build cooking fires. The aroma of bacon and eggs frying hung heavy in the humid, still mountain air. Imogene spotted him first and ran to meet him. When she held a hand up for him to take, he gripped it and swung her onto the saddle behind him.

Hugging the big man, she questioned, "Where did you go last night? I was worried sick. Jessie, too. She was just telling us about how you rescued her, the fight with Kills Fast and all."

"Did you tell her about your being taken by the medicine man?"

"No. She was talking so fast that I couldn't get a word in edgewise. That man with her, Jeek O'Grady, is an ape. He's dumb, Fargo. Really."

"And strong as an ox. Jeek doesn't know his own strength. He is dangerous, Imogene. Stay away from him. Have you seen Hilary's—I mean Jessie's father?"

"Yes. He's a quiet man. Lost a lot of weight since I last saw him. Hair, too. These people are wondering what to do, where to go. The wagon master ran off without putting up a fight. The sorry so-and-so. Did you find her naked?"

"Of course, Imogene."

"Are you sure the medicine man's dead?"

"If he isn't, he's the first person walking around with a cut gizzard and a seared back. Yes, Kills Fast is dead."

Jessie stood as they rode up. Imogene dropped to the ground, but Fargo remained in the saddle to make a head count and scan their faces. They were in two groups surrounding cooking fires. Fargo counted twenty-seven survivors, twelve in one group, fifteen in the other. Most were still recovering from the Cheyenne medicine man's brutal attack. He asked, "How many died?"

"Eight," Philo/Kurt answered. "We buried them."
He pointed to the line of mud-soaked mounds off the trail.

Fargo saw three were the length of youngsters. He shook his head sorrowfully. He moved the Ovaro to stand between the two groups so all could hear. "You people want to turn back and go to St. Louis?" He figured Hilary would be the first to answer.

Instead, John did. John stuttered, "N-n-no! We, we, I, I must g-g-get to San Fran-Francisco as soon as p-p-possible."

The man's stutter confirmed what Abigail had told Fargo about his mannerisms. It was now crystal-clear to him that he faced John Tuggle. Moreover, he now knew the man had the money with him. Fargo looked questioningly at the others.

After exchanging nervous glances with one another, one of the women said, "I think Josiah Dunlop spoke for us all when he said we should go on."

Fargo then asked, "Any of you know the way and what to expect up ahead?"

John answered, the stutter suddenly gone, "No, but last night before the storm we discussed it. The trail is well-worn. We can find our way."

The last part was true. Others had found their way to California, but not without paying terrible penalties. Without a seasoned, knowledgeable guide most had perished. Fargo knew about whom he spoke when he said, "Half of you will not survive the last eight hundred miles, which is about how far you still have to go. If the Indians don't get you, then the desert in Western Utah Territory will. And Josiah"—he paused to look at the banker, then continued—"you can expect to find lengthy stretches where the California Trail simply does not exist. Oh, yes, you can follow the sun and eventually come to California, but not before getting lost many times and wandering aimlessly."

He paused to let his words sink in, then said, "Now, I'll lead you folks, but only if you agree to obey my rules and do what I say without any backchat or griping. I promise you that from this pass until we reach the Sierras, it will be a brutal, demanding journey. I'll give you a few minutes to think it over and talk about what I just said." He dismounted and stepped to a woman holding a frying pan filled with bacon.

She handed him a plate, put two strips of fried bacon on it, then looked at his size and added four more strips. Another woman put three basted eggs on the plate. A third added four delicious-smelling biscuits and a glob of butter. Fargo took the plate of food and sat apart from the crowd. He watched their expressions and listened to them discuss the matter while he ate.

The banker became their spokesman. He came to Fargo and said, "We accept your offer. Everybody agrees to do what you say."

Fargo glanced at Chad and the two detectives. "Everybody? None objected?"

"Certainly, there were a few dissenting votes. But in the end they came around. How much money is required for your services?"

"Not a penny," Fargo replied. "I was going to California anyway."

Nodding, the banker said, "By the way, I want to thank you for rescuing my dau—" he caught himself in time to trap the forming word, then stuttered, "M-M-Miss Jes-Jessie from those s-s-savages."

"Think nothing of it, Josiah. I would have killed the man anyhow. He's been attacking wagon trains on South Pass for years. Molesting, terrorizing, and then killing white female captives on a regular basis."

The banker nodded once, turned, and walked away.

Fargo called Imogene to him. She came and sat beside him. He told her, "Ask Jeek and Barney and the three men standing with them to come see me. But before you do, would you fetch me a cup of coffee to wash down these biscuits?"

Imogene got up and brought Fargo a steaming cup of coffee. He watched as she approached Jeek and the others. They looked at Fargo briefly before walking to him. All but Jeek squatted to hear what he had to say.

"Now, men," Fargo began, "here's how it is and how you figure into my scheme of things." Even Chad became more attentive. Fargo continued his monologue, "I know that you, Philo, Brandon, and Stark have taken on new identities." He paused when Barney visibly stiffened and cut frowning glances to the three men, then picked up where he left off. "Oh, no, Barney, they are not what they proposed to be. Philo and Brandon, or Kurt and George, are private detectives. Chad, or Orville—I don't know what he is, not that it matters."

Jeek interrupted to say, "George, you told me back in that saloon in Kearney your name was George Taylor. Why did you lie to me?"

"No," Brandon/George began the confession, "my name is Brandon Sizemore. And, like Fargo said, I am a private detective. Philo and I are partners. I do believe Fargo has more to say." He looked questioningly at Fargo.

The big man grinned, took a sip of his coffee, then said, "While I don't know exactly what you fellows have planned; I do know it has something to do with a substantial amount of cash."

Barney looked at Brandon and Philo.

Jeek said, "What's sub—whatcha call it mean?"

Chad explained, "It means a whole lot."

Now Fargo lied, for no other purpose than achieving unity while he gained additional information. "Abigail Tuggle told me they took $175,000 from the bank. Hilary Tuggle told me where she and her father have it. A few moments ago John Tuggle offered me ten thousand dollars to get him to California safely. Though I told him okay, I plan to resteal the stolen money the instant these wagons roll into Carson Valley. Now, there's enough money to go around. I get the lion's share—fifty thousand—and you boys can divide the rest. That's only fair, seeing how I know where to lay hands on the cash. Without me, none of you would ever find it. So I suggest one or more of you stick close to me."

Jeek offered a concern, "What if they catch us stealing their money?"

"Well, Jeek, you and Barney can have the pleasure of killing them."

Chad hurried to add, "But not before I fuck her. Huh, big man—partner?"

"Be my guest," Fargo grunted. He looked at Philo, who was frowning.

Brandon spoke evenly when he looked at Fargo and said, "Abigail Tuggle told Philo and me $350,000 was missing from the bank."

Fargo faked shocked surprise. He said, "Well, now, Brandon, you just caught me in a lie. Can't blame me for trying. You'd done the same. All of you would have lied. Admit it."

Chad had apparently refigured the arithmetic. He said, "Lying to us is going to cost you the lion's share, big man. The way I figure it each man gets about $58,000. Right boys?"

Jeek nodded.

Fargo said, "What the hell. Done." Chad started to get up. Fargo pulled him back down and said, "The others might as well hear what I have to say to you. Fellows, Chad and I have had two fights. Once in St. Louis, once in Fort Kearney. Philo and Brandon witnessed the second one. In Keefer's Saloon back in St. Louis I beat the shit out of Stark. So, I won that one. We shot each other in the saloon at Kearney. That's a draw. He fixed it so I would go to jail. You won that one, Chad. Now we're even-Steven. I'll let bygones be bygones if you will. What do you say? I don't want to keep looking over my shoulder."

Stark smiled as he stood to say, "I don't fight my partners."

Fargo hoped he wouldn't agree to the standoff. He said, "From here on I'm going to call you all by your new names, Hilary and John, too. We don't want to let the cat out of the bag and give him or her any reason to become suspicious. Got that, Jeek?"

Jeek nodded and said, "How do you want me to kill her? Blow her brains out or use my dagger on her?"

"Uh, no mess, Jeek," Fargo muttered. "Choke her to death."

Brandon had apparently been thinking on something else also. He asked, "Did that fat, smelly bitch hire you, too? And, if so, what's the deal? How much are you getting?"

Fargo leveled with him. "She gave me five hundred. I'm to get five hundred more when I bring her husband and the money back to her. Abigail doesn't want her daughter returned. What did she pay you two?"

Philo answered, "Two fifty each and a promise of one thousand more upon delivery of the cash. Brandon asked, and she said she didn't want her husband or daughter back. Guess she changed her mind about him."

"Yeah, well, the way I got it figured she isn't going to get anything back." Fargo stood, emptied his cup of cold coffee on the ground, then gave them their marching orders. "Kurt, you ride at the head of the column. You, George, bring up the rear. Orville rides swing, and Imogene and I will ride point, scout the trail, and look for trouble. Imogene will relay any messages to Kurt. Kurt can tell the others. Now, let's shove those fire-gutted wagons off the trail, then head out."

"What about the extra oxen?" Jeek wanted to know.

"Divide them up and trail them behind the wagons," Fargo answered. "We'll eat them one at a time."

They walked to the wagons. On the way Fargo said, "You two detectives and Orville stay next to me. Barney, you and Jeek walk ahead and stand with Josiah and Jessie. They will wonder what we talked about. Tell them I was choosing my crew and going over what is to be done. Think you can remember that, Jeek?"

When Jeek's eyes started darting left and right, Barney grabbed his arm and hurried away. Fargo halted his men short of the crowd and said, "First, I've selected these three men to be my crew. Do what they say. Second, unhitch those oxen pulling the burned-out wagons. Divide them and trail them to those that are left. Third, all men and strong boys are to move the burned wagons off the pass so others coming this way will have room to get around them. Remove all sound wheels and other hardware from the burned wagons and put them in the provision wagon. As for you ladies and young, pretty girls, you know what to do without me telling."

A fleshy, older woman with her arms folded at her bosom muttered, "Wash the dishes and cooking utensils."

That broke the tension. Laughing, they moved to carry out Fargo's instructions.

He approached Imogene and said, "Your job is to ride point with me." A smile spread across her shining face. Fargo went to help with the teams.

In short order, the oxen were divided and tied to the rear of the wagons, the four fire-swept wagons muscled to the north side of the pass, and their wheels stowed in the provisions Conestoga. Fargo looked at the women, all of whom were in their places on driver's seats. Knocking the coal smudges off his shirt, he told Kurt, "Head them out, partner. Money waits for us in Carson Valley."

Imogene sat astride her Indian pony next to the Ovaro. She smiled as Fargo got into his saddle, then asked, "What's a point?"

"Follow me and you will learn," he answered, and dug the heels of his boots into the pinto's flanks.

They rode off South Pass at a gallop.

11

The five wagons, with Jeek and Hilary in the lead, crept through mountain valleys, high country meadows, and gorgeous forests. Fargo took them along the Little Sandy's crystal-clear waters and the Sandy River itself, always moving toward the southwest corner of Wyoming Territory. In midafternoon on the fourth day from South Pass, the wagons forded the Sandy. There Fargo halted for the night. A second ox was slaughtered and butchered. By sunset the womenfolk had steaks and roasts on their fires. Fritz Ubey played his guitar and sang while men and smaller children sat listening with faraway looks in their eyes.

Fargo and Imogene took their bedding to a grassy knoll a short distance downstream of the wagons. A quarter moon shone bright. So did the planet Venus near the tip of the moon's lower arc.

After a few minutes Barney walked up to them and squatted. Following Fargo's gaze to the moon and Venus, he said, "Pretty sight, isn't it, Fargo? Hate to disturb you, but the women said for me to tell you two the steaks are ready." He glanced at Imogene.

She rose and said, "I'll go get it. I know you have something to say to Fargo."

Barney watched her go down the grassy slope before saying, "Something's up, Fargo."

"Oh? What, specifically?"

"Don't know. Can't put my finger on it." Barney sat before continuing, "Today, Jessie changed seats with me, told me to ride with Jeek for a while. That's the first time since St. Louis that she and Josiah have ridden alone together. And another thing. Orville rides up to Kurt and they talk, then Orville drops back to ride next to George, and they talk."

"How long has that been going on?"

"Started just today."

"May mean nothing. Let me know if it happens again tomorrow. But you're right about the banker and his daughter. She seems almost civil since we left South Pass. Does Jeek have anything to say about the change in her mood?"

"Yes, he noticed it, too. He said she told him she was never so scared of anyone as she was of that medicine man who raped her. Jeek is of the opinion that he took her down a notch or two, knocked her off her high horse. What do you reckon is in the wind?"

"Don't rightly know. It could have something to do with you and Jeek, though."

"Like what?"

"Like when, where, and how to dispose of you two."

"You mean kill us?" Barney's shock was genuine.

"While it's none of my business, I am a mite curious to know how much they are paying you two on this trip."

"Five hundred apiece. Why? What's that got to do with them planning to kill us? Hell, they wouldn't miss five hundred."

"Does that amount include your killing those two people back in Chicago? You and Jeek did kill them, didn't you?"

Fargo thought Barney would deny any knowledge, but the man fooled him when he confessed, as though it happened every day. "Oh, yeah, me and Jeek killed them, all right. Right there in the bank. I told the whore a rich man would pay her one hundred dollars to suck him off. I told the drunk with her that Hilary—I didn't use her right name, though—wanted to suck him while she watched the whore sucking the rich man. A promise of a hundred for each of them made it easy for me to take them to the bank."

"Did Hilary and John see you kill them?"

"Hell, yes. I'm nobody's fool. I made them watch. I laid the drunk's guts wide open. Hell, he was so liquored up that he didn't even know his guts was spilling out on the floor. Jeek cut the whore's throat. Then we put them in Hilary's and John's chairs to make it look like they was him and her when the firemen found the bodies. I sloshed coal oil all around them on the floor. Hilary, John, and me went to the back door and waited for Jeek to strike a match."

"Did the three of you have the money?"

"No, never saw the money."

Fargo believed he knew the answer to his next two questions. "How did you get to St. Louis?"

"John had a coach and team of horses parked behind the bank. We went in it."

"What did you and Jeek do to kill time while John and Hilary made arrangements for the Conestogas?"

"When we wasn't drinking in the saloon, we was sleeping it off. John paid for everything. We talked him into paying an extra hundred apiece for killing the drunk and the whore."

Fargo was willing to bet Abigail's money that the stolen money was hidden under a false floor on one of the two Conestogas. He asked, "When did you learn about the bank money?"

"On South Pass. From you."

So, Fargo thought, I was wrong about Philo and Brandon. They kept it quiet when they met Jeek and Barney in the saloon back in Ft. Kearney. They probably didn't even mention it to Chad Stark. Fargo saw Imogene coming. He hurried to finish the conversation. "I'll tell you why I think they plan to murder you and Jeek."

Barney edged closer.

"They have to dispose of you because you two are the only other ones who know the truth about what happened in that bank."

"Huh, never thought of it that way. I see what you mean. Just goes to show that you can't trust anyone."

"That's right, Barney."

"What's right?" Imogene asked as she walked up.

"Barney and I were discussing the wind. He told me it blew mostly out of the west in these parts. I told him he was right. That steak smells delicious. Hand it over."

Barney stood and thanked Fargo for telling him what he did, then turned and headed for the wagons.

Fargo and Imogene ate in silence. Later, when the cooking fires burned low, they made love while listening to Fritz strum the guitar. Afterward, Imogene nestled her head in the crook of Fargo's shoulder and they drifted to sleep, him wondering what in blazes Stark was up to. The man would force him to kill him before it was over. Fargo was sure of that.

Sunsets gave way to sunrises, rains came and went, Blades Fork spilled into Muddy Creek. The small wagon train of settlers, murderers, thieves, and crooks left Wyoming Territory without knowing it and entered the Utah Territory panhandle. The Trailsman was in his element, the natural environment, his castle of streams, forests, and humbling mountains. He led the wagons through magnificent corridors in the Wasatch Range and followed the Hastings Cutoff in the California Trail, which went around the southern end of the Great Salt Lake. After snaking through the Lakeside Mountains, Fargo halted the wagons on the eastern rim of the Great Salt Desert. Gone for the moment were the lush green foliage and cool, refreshing streams, instantly replaced by shimmering heat waves that spawned dust devils.

The settlers went about their evening chores while watching their first desert sunset. The dying heat waves highly magnified the huge fireball that, as it met the horizon, appeared to melt and elongate at the bottom. The worst was yet to come.

Subsequent to putting Fargo wise to Hilary and John getting together, and Chad getting with Philo and Brandon Sizemore, Barney had reported the men got together on four additional occasions, and Hilary and her father had talked two more times. Then, as though final decisions had been made, everything reverted back to normal.

The detectives, trained in keeping a person under

close surveillance without the person knowing it, kept close tabs on Fargo and Imogene whenever they came off point and joined the wagons. The Trailsman noticed that they worked in shifts during the night. One always stayed awake to keep an eye on him and Imogene. Hilary became moody, bitchy, and prone to be argumentative.

Through guarded questions put to Barney, the big man learned that whenever John and Hilary rode together, she always went to his wagon, not him to hers. Accordingly, Fargo deduced the false floor was in John's wagon. Jeek O'Grady and Barney Ruttman could prowl and probe her wagon all they wanted to when she was gone and wouldn't find the cash.

Sitting at the fire, Fargo told everybody to come closer, he had something to say. They crowded around the fire. He said, "Try to stay awake tonight. Sleep tomorrow. All day if you can. I want you and the teams fully rested, because we start across this stretch of desert when the sun next goes down. It will be cool then and the full moon will be out. We should make excellent time in a night crossing.

"For your information—I know you are curious— we are about seventy five miles from the Western Utah Territory border and about 375 miles from Carson Valley.

"The southern cutoff we've been taking since South Pass is shorter than the main trail, and more brutal, but you're a tough lot. We'll make it. In time, we will rejoin the California Trail, then you will view wonders the likes of which you won't believe, some good, some not. You think this desert we are about to cross looks desolate and harsh; wait till you see the next one. I don't mean to frighten you, but to prepare you. Any questions?" Hearing none, he suggested Fritz get out his guitar and entertain everybody.

Fritz strummed the desert night away. At dawn the settlers began retiring inside or under the wagons. Fargo made a shade arbor out of a large square of canvas for him and Imogene to sleep under.

In midafternoon Fargo awakened, then sat and

drank coffee while waiting for the sun to go down. As the red rim of the sun disappeared over the flat horizon, he mounted up. Riding point was not necessary on this terrain, so he and Imogene rode alongside Philo.

Six days later only Fargo knew they had crossed into Western Utah Territory. The Pequop Mountains loomed ahead. They were negotiated, as were the Independence. Finally a meaningful source of water came into view: the serpentinelike Humboldt River. The females went upstream from the wagons, the males downstream. For the better part of two hours everybody bathed, then bathed again. Refreshed, their spirits picked up. It didn't last long.

Following either bank of the meandering Humboldt was simply out of the question. Fargo had the wagoneers ford it time and time again, until they became expert at doing it. Still, they lost one Conestoga to the swirling water. Haddie Locke, a four-year-old girl, drowned when the wagon turned on its side and was swept away. Haddie was the first to die since leaving South Pass. There would be more.

The Humboldt became increasingly brackish. Thirsty oxen became uncontrollable. They didn't know their unquenchable thirst was bloating, poisoning them. Oxen died. The Humboldt did, too. It simply evaporated in the desert and formed a sink of salt. Two more people perished, cutting their numbers to twenty-four in four wagons. The crucible of the desert was taking its toll.

Fargo halted the wagons at the Humboldt Sink and called everybody to him. "Folks," he began, "the next eighty miles will be the hardest. Your mettle is going to be tested in the caldron of this desert, where the temperatures soar to unmerciful heights. Seven days of living in hell is what you can expect. Those who survive will know they beat all odds. Those who want to turn back best do it now. Any takers?"

"We've come too far to turn back now," Fritz said. And he spoke for them all.

"Okay, then," Fargo said. "You'll want to shed your clothes. I'm telling you not to do it. Keep covered. As a matter of fact, wear something on your head and cover your face. All you men keep your shirt sleeves rolled down. Trap your sweat. It will keep you cooler than you might imagine. Drink as little water as you can. I dare say the barrels will run empty before we see the Sierras." He told them what they needed to know. Nothing more was to be said. He led them into the torture chamber.

On the first day two oxen died. With those being trailed long since slaughtered and butchered, two less increased the burden on those remaining. One team of two now had to pull one Conestoga. On the third day those two died, and the heat made a raving lunatic out of Mary Ellison. She died during the night. The teamless wagon was abandoned. Fargo crowded twelve settlers into the three that were left: John's, Hilary's, and the one carrying the spare wheels and other items. He, Imogene, and the rest rode their horses or walked.

The morning of day four found three oxen dead. The provision wagon was abandoned and settlers began taking turns walking.

During the next day two of Jobe and Lily Pearson's children suffered heat strokes and died. Their deaths dropped the number in the group to twenty-one.

Day five killed three more oxen and Willie Jones. Hilary's wagon was left sitting on the desert floor. She rode double with Chad. Jeek joined the crowd walking. It was down to John's wagon, and Fargo noticed his nervousness. John refused to walk. Fargo knew why.

On the morning of the seventh day the Sierras appeared as blue haze on the distant horizon. The surviving oxen must have smelled moisture in the air for even they visibly strengthened and picked up speed.

At high noon they were in sight of Hall's Station. Fargo heard gunfire erupt and halted the bedraggled procession. He told them, "I'm going ahead to check on that gunfire. You people wait here till I come back. Philo, I'm putting you in charge. See to it that they obey." He rode away at a gallop.

As he approached the mouth of the ravine, the gunfire grew louder. He saw shacks and what appeared to be Chinese coolies scampering to safety inside them. He dismounted at the largest shack. Three sides of it were hinged to raise. Four feet of wainscot ran across the front and down both sides of the shack. The hinged portion of each wall was propped up by poles and formed a shady, overhanging roof. Fargo went inside. Coolies cowered in the shadows of the smoky room. Tables and chairs were scattered about.

Fargo asked, "Do any of you speak English?" He pulled one of the wide-eyed, trembling coolies to his feet. The little fellow gasped but said nothing.

A short, fat Chinese wearing an apron sat in a dark corner. He announced, "They don't speak English. I do."

Fargo stepped to him, told him to stand, that he wasn't there to hurt anybody, then said, "Tell them what I just said."

The fat man quickly made the translation, then looked at the big man and said, "My name is Fa-ting. I'm the cook. They are humble ditch-diggers for boss-man Reese. We don't want trouble. We don't make trouble for anybody. Bad rice in Gold Canyon." He glanced toward the door.

"What's going on out there, Fa-ting?"

"Many bad men came to Hall's Station. Shoot everybody. Bad rice. Coolies throw down picks and shovels. Run home. Much bad rice."

Fargo moved to the doorway and looked out. Hall's Station had grown since he last saw it. Structures fairly dotted both sides and tops of the ravine. And the Chinese were new. He listened to the sporadic shooting a few seconds, then stepped to the Ovaro, eased into the saddle, and rode up the ravine at a walk. What had Fa-ting called it, Gold Canyon?

As he passed a large two-story house—it and the picket fence surrounding it appeared recently built—a woman pushed the front screen door partway open and beckoned him to her. He nodded, angled the stallion toward the picket fence. Hitching the Ovaro next to the two horses tied to pickets, he saw bodies of two men dressed in miner's clothes sprawled in the dirt of the front yard. Fargo pushed the gate open, took a few paces, and paused to take a closer look at the two men.

The woman spoke in a loud whisper, "Hurry, mister."

The men were dead. One from a head wound, the other riddled in the back. Fargo halted with one boot on the wide steps and said, "What's the problem, ma'am?"

She glanced up the ravine, saying, "It's dangerous out there in the open. Come inside."

He stepped around her and went inside the house, which he immediately recognized as being a whorehouse. Four shapely young females lounged on sofas and in wing chairs. They eyed him like felines about to pounce. A wiry black man rested his elbows on the short bar at one side of the spacious room. He shot Fargo a toothy smile.

The woman latched the screen door and moved to the bar. "Fix me a gin, Toady. What are you drinking, big'un?" She glanced at Fargo.

"Bourbon."

She turned to face him and rested her back against the bar. "I'm Margot Zimmer, the owner and madam of this establishment. You're new in Gold Canyon, aren't you? Have you come to mine for gold or silver? There's plenty of both."

"Not a miner, ma'am," he said, and stepped to the bar. Toady handed him a glass of bourbon.

"Not a miner?" Margot echoed. "Well, what are you?"

He told her about the settlers waiting a short distance from Hall's Station.

"Hall's Station?" she snorted. "I haven't heard that in a long time. You haven't been here since Pancake Comstock discovered that blue stuff in his diggings was silver?"

"No," Fargo admitted, "I haven't been this way in several years. What are the coolies doing here?"

"They are digging a water ditch to the placer mines in Gold Canyon. John Reese brought them in. This part of Gold Canyon is called Chinatown. Silver City is a little way up the canyon and Gold Hill farther up, at the head of it."

Their conversation was interrupted by hoofbeats pounding to a halt at the picket fence. A man shouted, "Free pussy, boys! All you want! I get the madam."

The four whores instantly fled up the staircase. Toady ducked behind the bar.

Margot told Fargo. "Go out the back door. I'll handle them."

Fargo shook his head. Withdrawing his Colt, he moved to the screen door and watched three rough-looking men file through the gate. Without noticing him standing there, one tried to yank open the latched screen.

Fargo muttered, "We're closed for the day."

The man jerked back a few paces and drew his six-gun. Fargo fired through the screen. Blood appeared on the fellow's shirt in the heart area. The impact of the bullet catapulted him off the porch. His friends leapt off the porch and ran toward the fence, firing randomly at the house. Slugs chewed into the front of the house next to the door. Fargo shot one of the men in his left thigh as he vaulted the pickets. They mounted up on the run and rode up the canyon, their horses in a dead run.

Margot appeared behind Fargo. Looking around him, she whispered, "Now you've done it. They will go tell Zack and the others."

"Oh? And who or what is this Zack and the others?"

"Zack Conklin is the leader of a gang of rowdies from San Francisco. He and the sixteen of them rode into the canyon yesterday evening. They took control of the Gold Hill first, then moved down to Chinatown at the mouth. Killing, looting, raping, tearing the towns apart. Zack's headquarters is the saloon in Silver City."

Fargo made no comment. He slipped the latch on the screen door and went to get his Sharps. When he came back, he slouched on a sofa.

Margot asked, "Didn't you hear me, big'un? I said Zack and the others would come for you."

"Lock all the doors and windows, ma'am. This is as good of a place as any to fight from."

Margot started pulling him to his feet. She said, "Oh, no, you're not wrecking my house. Zack will murder me, my girls, and Toady for harboring you. I know he will. You're leaving here. Please go, now."

Fargo heaved his bulk off the sofa and moved to the door. He glanced at the coolie's shacks, then shifted his gaze up the ravine. Finally, he muttered, "I'll be back." He swung the door open.

Margot watched him go to the Ovaro and mount up. She yelled, "Go into the desert. They will kill you if you don't."

The Trailsman had no intention of doing what she suggested. He reined the stallion and headed for Silver City to have it out with Zack Conklin and his gang of butchers. It was the only way to open the way for the tired settlers to leave the parched desert.

He skirted Silver City, came behind a building, and sat easy in the saddle while peering around its corner to watch the saloon. In the street in front of the saloon lay three twisted bodies of miners. At the hitching rails of the saloon stood twenty saddled horses. He watched five men come through the double doors, mount up, and head in the direction of Chinatown. Fargo dismounted and sat in the shade of the building to wait.

Twenty minutes passed before he heard hoofbeats on the street. He leaned and looked around the corner. The five men were dismounting. He watched them enter the saloon, then Fargo pulled back and plucked a blade of grass. He chewed on it while waiting for the sun to go down.

Sporadic gunfire came from up the canyon. He reckoned part of the gang was still bringing around miners on Gold Hill. He wanted all the gang together in one place, so he waited.

About four o'clock he heard the coolies start screaming. He thought he heard Hilary's screams shrill through them. If he was correct, it meant the settlers had arrived at Chinatown. He stood and listened more closely. There was no doubt about it: he would know Hilary's scream anywhere. But why were she and the Chinese screaming? The gang wasn't anywhere near Chinatown.

As he stepped to the Ovaro to go investigate, Philo rode over the top of the ravine and came to him. He watched Barney, Jeek, Chad and Brandon top the rise, following right behind Philo. He asked Philo, "What's up? Why did you leave the settlers?"

"We got worried when you didn't come back, so we rode in to see about you, what with all the gunfire and all."

"A gang—sixteen men—is terrorizing the miners and townspeople," Fargo rushed to explain. "What's all the commotion at the mouth of the canyon? I heard Hilary screaming."

Philo glanced toward the noise. "Don't rightly know. We left her and the others right where they were. They must have got tired of waiting, too. A gang you say?"

"Yes. I'm waiting for them all to collect in the saloon across the street."

"Oh? Then what do you intend to do? Rush them with all your guns blazing?"

"Something like that."

"With you dead, we won't know how to find the money. Before leaving, we made everyone get out of the wagon, then all four of us gave it a good going over. Where is it, Fargo, partner?"

"It isn't there," Fargo lied. "And you're right. Without me, you won't find the money. I told all of you that a long time ago. So, you men best pitch in with me and help fight this gang."

Brandon asked, "What, exactly, do you have in mind? You do have a plan?"

"Of sorts," Fargo began. "Since you men are here, I've changed it. As I now see it, we set up an ambush in Chinatown."

"Chinatown?" Chad interrupted.

"You saw the shacks at the mouth of the canyon?" Fargo inquired.

"Didn't notice," Chad replied. "I saw a big house with three horses hitched to a picket fence."

"You saw Chinatown," Fargo continued. "The house is a whorehouse. Margo Zimmer is the madam. Three of you go to the whorehouse and two hide out among the coolies' shacks. I'll go inside the saloon—"

Fargo was interrupted by the sounds of riders approaching the saloon. He moved to the corner of the building and watched five men dismount and go inside. Turning back to the fivesome, he picked up where he left off. "I'll go inside the saloon and shoot as many of the gang as I can before backing off. Then I'll ride for Chinatown. I'll swing close by the whorehouse. The three of you there can thin them out even more. Then I'll join the two at the shacks.

"The gang won't be expecting anything. They've already killed or sent into hiding all the townspeople and miners who put up a fight. The element of surprise will be with me, then you men."

He watched five heads nod.

Chad said, "Who wants to be in the whorehouse with me?"

Barney and Jeek raised hands.

Fargo told Philo and Brandon, "The largest shack is where the coolies eat. I'll take it. You men fight from behind the ones on either side of it. Now, saddle up and get going. I'll count to twenty-five, then do my part."

When they left, Fargo mounted up. He started the count as he went around the corner. He finished as he rode through the double doors, his Colt firing hot lead.

In rapid order he shot three of the gang standing with six others at the bar, then he swung the Colt onto those sitting at the tables and emptied the cylinder at them. Fargo wheeled the Ovaro and rode back outside. A barrage of bullets tore into the woodwork behind him. The Ovaro charged down the street. Fargo quickly reloaded the Colt.

Between Silver City and Chinatown he met a sizable

band of pony-mounted Piaute. Confused by the big man's audacity, they divided, one group taking to high ground on the right, the other charging up the slope of the ravine on the left.

Within seconds he passed the picket fence. Not three, but nine horses were hitched to it. Imogene's Indian pony stood in the middle of them. Chad waved from an open window upstairs. Barney and Jeek stood at two others. Brandon stood in the open doorway, and Philo at a downstairs, raised window.

Zack's gang rode in a tight pack no more than fifty yards behind him. Fargo maintained a straight course to bring the gang within firing range of Philo and the others in the whorehouse.

He looked toward the coolies' shacks. Tuggle's Conestoga stood in front of the cook's shack. Pony-mounted Piaute warriors shot arrows as they circled the cluster of shacks and the Conestoga. Fargo swerved, headed straight for the fat cook's shack.

He heard Chad and the others open fire and glanced behind. Riders were toppling off their horses and tumbling onto the ground.

Boldly, he penetrated the circling warriors and reined the Ovaro to an abrupt halt between the Conestoga and Fa-ting's shack. As the stallion squatted, Fargo withdrew his Sharps from its saddle case and dismounted. He ran and dived through the wide opening at the front of the shack.

Chairs and tables crashed onto the floor as he hurtled into them. Bullets and arrows thudded into the shack while others hammered into walls above the screaming coolies. Fargo crawled to the opening and peered out.

Zack's gang, what was left of it, mingled with the Piaute. Fargo had many easy targets to shoot at. He went to work on the gang first.

The Sharps thundered twice. Two gang members fell to the ground, red spreading across the fronts of their shirts. He saw a Piaute arrow drop another one.

Swinging left to right, the Trailsman shot three more of Zack's gang from their saddles, two in the head, one in the heart. He drew his Colt and emptied it on red targets. Piaute warriors bit the dust. Fargo reloaded the Colt and resumed firing.

The Piaute began breaking off and heading for open country in the desert. Fargo ducked behind the partition to reload. He had inserted one cartridge into the cylinder when a bull of a man burst through the door, yelling in a gravely voice, "Nobody does this to Zack Conklin! Where is the man riding the black-and-white horse?" He looked at the coolies cowering at the back wall.

"Over here," Fargo answered nonchalantly.

Zack turned and fired. The bullet went where Fargo's heart would have been had he been standing.

The Colt barked once. The bullet slammed into Zack's left shoulder. The force of it spun him around. During the spin, Fargo drew and threw his Arkansas toothpick. The blade buried hilt-deep in the middle of Zack's chest. He fell backward. As he fell, the index finger on his gun hand pulled the trigger three times—the slugs stitched an evenly spaced pattern of holes in the ceiling.

Fargo calmly resumed reloading. He stepped to the open doorway and looked out. The last two men in Zack's gang were hightailing it toward the desert. He moved to Zack and retrieved his stiletto. Wiping the bloody blade on Zack's trousers, he looked at Fa-ting and said, "The Indians and the gang are gone."

Fa-ting rose from his hunker. "Bad rice, boss big man. Bad rice."

Fargo stepped outside and went to the Conestoga. He found Hilary hiding under the driver's seat. "You can come out now, ma'am. It's all over."

She squirmed out and looked around. Focusing on him, she spat, "You were supposed to protect us!"

"Are you hurt, ma'am? Where are the others?"

"No, I'm not hurt, no thanks to you. And I don't know where the others are. They started walking almost immediately after you rode away. Josiah Dunlop and I stayed where you said."

Fargo looked inside the wagon. "Where is Josiah?"

"Dead," she answered, finality in the tone, then explained, "The savages attacked us on their way here. They killed him."

"Where's his body?"

"Out there." She pointed toward the desert. "I buried Josiah, then drove here. This is as far as I got when the savages attacked again."

Fargo climbed up and sat beside her. Before he could slap the whip on the oxen's backs, Chad and the others rode up. Chad eyed him suspiciously as he said, "Where do you think you're going . . . partner?"

Fargo ignored him and asked Philo, "Where are the settlers?"

Philo answered, "At the whorehouse."

Chad drew his revolver and aimed it at Fargo's head. "Get down on the ground," he snarled. "Both of you."

Fargo dropped to the ground and extended his hand to Hilary. She knocked it aside and jumped to the ground.

Chad said, "Use two fingers, Hilary, to take his Colt out of his holster, then put the gun on the ground and kick it under my horse." When she hesitated, Chad bellowed, "Goddammit, I told you to get his gun. Move!"

She removed the Colt from its holster and booted it under the horse. Then she said, "You called me Hilary. My name's Jessie."

"No it isn't," Brandon interjected. "Your name is Hilary Tuggle. You're from Chicago. We're here to get the money you and your father stole from the bank. Where is he?"

"Dead," she said. "Killed by Indians when they attacked us." She went on to explain the circumstances.

Chad said, "Okay, partners, tear that fucking wagon apart. I'll keep them covered while you do."

Jeek climbed inside the Conestoga and began passing two picks and a sledgehammer out to the others. Fargo watched them start dismantling the wagon. Philo used a knife to cut the canvas top away. Fargo saw the oxen were restless from the racket going on behind them. He judged the diving distance to his Colt, then whistled loudly.

The Ovaro sprang into action instantly as the oxen lurched forward. Those on the wagon lost their balance. Fargo dived beneath Chad's skittish horse. The stallion ran and bumped Chad's horse. Fargo rolled out into the open on the far side. His first shot knocked Chad from the saddle, a hunk of his head missing. He got Barney in the chest with his second bullet, Philo in the neck with the next. Standing, Fargo stalked the other two, who were crouched behind the left side of the partially destroyed wagon. He shot Jeek in the head when the man poked it up to look. Then the team panicked and ran.

Fargo grabbed the left side of the wagon and swung his legs over it. Brandon fired, but the jostling wagon caused him to miss. He fired and missed again. Fargo lunged for him, then stood and pulled Brandon upright. They toppled over the back of the wagon. Both lost their guns. Fargo withdrew his stiletto. Brandon scrambled to his feet and dived at Fargo. Fargo fell onto his back and aimed the Arkansas toothpick upward. Brandon's free-falling, deadweight body caught the blade in the stomach and ripped it open. Bloody intestines spilled out. Fargo rolled away in time to avoid the falling body.

Fargo rose, wiped the blade clean on Brandon's pants leg, then picked up his Colt and reloaded it. Hilary was on her knees, sobbing. He went to her and pulled her to stand. She began hitting his chest, yelling, "Leave me alone, you bastard!"

Grabbing her wrist, he assured her, "I'm not going to kill you, Hilary, although you deserve to die for what you and John did."

Startled, she gasped, "You know?"

She allowed Fargo to cradle her in his arms, even curled an arm around his neck. She was calm now. The still before the storm, Fargo thought, but said, "Yes, Hilary, I know. I met your mother in Chicago. She told me all about the bank and where she thought you two had gone. In my hip pocket is the letter from Horatio Arnold in San Francisco to your father."

The Ovaro followed him to the whorehouse. The oxen had stopped in the road by the picket fence. Fargo paused to look at the bed of the wagon. Hilary watched him scan the severely broken false bottom. He knew the money wasn't there, but looked anyhow. He carried her through the gate, up the path to the front door before lowering her to her feet. He held the door open for her to enter first.

Inside, he saw all the settlers. He said, "Folks, the Piaute have left, so that menace is past. You saw Zack Conklin's gang ride by a short time ago. Those who weren't killed from this whor—place of business were subsequently dispatched in a most deadly way. So they no longer are a bother to you or these good citizens. And I had to shoot all of my crew also. So you won't be seeing them again. Toady, fix me a bourbon."

As he stepped to the bar, he noticed Hilary eyed him in a strange sort of way. Her eyes darted left and right, as though her mind raced. He wondered what the woman was up to now. Toady handed him a glass half-filled with amber liquid. Imogene appeared next to him. She had a most puzzled expression on her face. When she tried a grin that didn't work out, Fargo asked, "What's on your mind, Imogene? Bad news?"

She lowered her gaze and muttered, "Oh, God, I thought I could tell you. Now that we're face to face, I can't."

"Spit it out, woman. What's bothering you?"

"Promise you won't hit me? Or think I'm ungrateful?"

"What is it, Imogene? No, I won't hit you. I don't hit females."

She started stammering, "I, I, er, uh, I—"

Margot stepping close to them interrupted Imogene. The madam explained, "She's trying to tell you that she wants to work for me."

"Oh, God," Imogene groaned.

Fargo kissed her on the forehead. "Imogene, you'll make a fine whore," he said.

Rapture spread across Imogene's face. Embracing him, she whispered, "You can have me anytime you want, and as long as you desire, for free." She glanced at Margot for her approval.

"Well, I wouldn't go so far as to say free," Margot began, smiling, "but half-price is in order for what he did today. The drinks will be free, though." Margot took Imogene by the elbow and said, "Come along, Talbot. That buckskin dress has to go. I'll fix you up with something new and pretty."

Fargo watched Margot lead Imogene away. As they passed Hilary, he noticed she was staring at him. Their eyes met. She smiled and came to him. "I've heard barracuda smile like that just before they take a big bite out of a tuna," Fargo began wryly. "Am I your tuna?"

Hilary didn't answer. She hooked an arm in his and led him to an upstairs bedroom. She closed the door and flattened her back against it. Raising on tiptoes, Hilary kissed him openmouthed. He heard her lock the door, then watched her shimmy out of her dress.

Looking into his lake-blue eyes, she whispered, "Take me, big man. Take me now. I owe you a lot, and I pay my debts." She circled an arm around his neck and kissed him again.

He shoved her undergarments down on her hips. A quick twist by Hilary and the clothing fell to the floor. He undid the hooks on the back of her bodice and removed the garment. Holding the kiss, she removed his gun belt and lowered it to the floor, then released his belt buckle and opened his fly. Fargo's Levi's slipped down to his knees.

Hilary clamped her right foot on his buttocks, then swung the left up and locked it with the left. Fargo's hard member met her slickened opening. When he gripped her buttocks, she clung to his shoulders. He pressed the little barracuda hard against the door and thrust. Hilary gasped, "Oh! Oh! Aaugh! Nice . . . so nice." She started bouncing on it, driving him ever deeper into the slippery sheath.

Fargo pulled on her buttocks and went in fully. She whimpered, "Oh, oh . . . yes, yes . . . so big, so good. Don't stop, big man." She twisted and thrust her left breast for him to take in his mouth. "Suck it, big man. Oh, yes, suck it hard."

He teased the nipple with his tongue, then slid to the right nipple and rolled it between his teeth. She mewed, childlike. "That feels so good, so good. Your tongue, it's setting me on fire." She squirmed, encouraging him to take the pillowy mound into his mouth and wiggling on his throbbing staff at the same time.

When he sucked on the breast, Hilary tensed, arched her back, and started biting on his ears and neck. He pulled on her buttocks. Inside deeply, he began a series of tiny thrusts that rubbed on the top of her tender slit. She gasped, "Oh, oh . . . that's so wonderful . . . heavenly. Oh, Fargo, don't stop . . . please make it last . . . forever." She started gulping. Her head lolled. She screamed, "Now, Fargo! Oh, my God! Come with me. Come with me."

He kept the rhythm as her hot tunnel seized him and squeezed, relaxed and tightened again. Hilary moaned her joy as he erupted. Her fingernails raked his shoulders and she dug her heels into his hard buttocks, forcing him not to withdraw. He felt her buttocks tighten under his grip and her lower charm mate firmly with the base of his throbbing, jerking length.

When Hilary had milked him dry, he lowered a hand to the waistband of his Levi's and raised them so he wouldn't trip and fall. Locked together, he carried Hilary and lowered her onto the bed.

She gazed up at him through drooped eyelids and gave him a smile of satisfaction. All acidity was gone from her tone of voice when she whispered, "I know I have been a pure bitch in the past, but you have changed all that. Fargo, you made me feel like a woman for the first time. I didn't know it could be this way, feel so good. The few men I have bedded left me unsatisfied. Stay with me, Fargo. I'll take care of you, provide all your wants and needs. Ours will be the good life. You will see."

Fargo had heard it many times before. Since it was coming from Hilary, he knew her offer wasn't made out of desire for his body, but out of necessity. She was trying to keep him close to her while she figured out what to do with him. He knew too much. That would never do. She had stood and watched two killings. That set a precedent. Watching a third—his— would be easy for the woman.

Buckling up, he said, "That's a splendid offer, Hilary, one that most men would be quick to accept. Not me. The city life is not to my liking." When she pouted, he suggested, "Align yourself with Margot Zimmer. This canyon is full of gold and silver. She can't mine it, but she can own the mine. With your head for business and her money, the two of you can go a long way, have the good life of which you speak. Fortunes are to be made in Carson Valley, Hilary. I suggest you grab one of them."

"I'll make it on my own, thank you. I don't need the madam of a whorehouse to help me."

"Have it your way," he replied dryly. But a seed had been planted in her mind, one that he knew would take root, sprout, grow, and bloom. He said, "I've been employed by your mother."

Surprised, she sat up and gasped, "Oh?"

"I'll report that I found you and John, that he was killed by Indians, and that you are safe in Carson Valley. My orders are not to bring you back to her."

"I wouldn't go back to Chicago for anything in the world, least of all to see my mother. I despise her. She has bullied me and my father for the last time. Yes, we took the money and burned the bank. It was little compensation for the misery she visited on us all these years. No, I wouldn't go back."

Fargo stepped to the door. Swinging his gun belt around his waist, he said, "Don't forget what I just suggested." He touched the brim of his hat, unlocked the door, and left her sitting, staring at him.

Downstairs he handed Fritz Ubey all that he had

left of Abigail Tuggle's advance money. "Take it, Fritz. Use the money as you see fit to get these settlers to their final destinations. The Conestoga out front is a wreck, but it can be repaired."

"That wagon belongs to Josiah, Mr. Fargo," Fritz replied. "He wouldn't take kindly to me confiscating it."

"Josiah is dead," Fargo began, "and I think his daughter, Jessie, won't mind. I think she'll be staying here." Turning to Margot, he said, "The woman has a business head, especially insofar as banking is concerned. Together, you two might very well end up owning a good part of this canyon. I suggest you give it a good try."

He shot her a wink, touched the brim of his hat, and went to his horse. He rode to the cook's shack and called Fa-ting outside. "Fa-ting, I'm leaving now. I apologize for making Chinatown a battlefield. The choice wasn't mine."

Several coolies came out of the shack and joined Fa-ting. After chattering briefly in Chinese to the fat cook, Fa-ting turned to Fargo and explained, "They say big boss man come look-see." He gestured for Fargo to dismount and follow them.

Fargo went with them to behind the shack adjacent to the cook's shack. They pointed to a man's body lying facedown next to the wall. Four arrows protruded from the man's back. Fargo rolled the body onto its side. The dead man was John Tuggle. Fargo concluded that he had run from the Conestoga in hopes of surviving, only to meet his death. Hilary didn't know that John Tuggle had really died. He decided she didn't need to know. When her father didn't show up, it would be easier for Hilary to do what Fargo had suggested. As a matter of fact, she would be forced to unite with Margot. He told Fa-ting, "Tell them to bury the body in an unmarked grave."

Walking back to the Ovaro, he told Fa-ting to have a coolie bring him a shovel.

The Trailsman intended to stop at John Tuggle's desert grave.

LOOKING FORWARD!

**The following is the opening
section from the next novel in the exciting
Trailsman series from Signet:**

**THE TRAILSMAN #112
THE DOOMSDAY WAGONS**

*They took the red man's name for
the land and he wrote his claim in blood.
Minnesota, 1860, the north country . . .*

The big man's lake-blue eyes narrowed as he guided
the magnificent black-and-white Ovaro through the
mountain ash. He peered through the flat clusters of
small white flowers to where the lone wagon rolled
along the flat land below the high ridge: one wagon,
a two-horse brace, and as far as he could see, a lone
driver. Again he caught the flash of full, thick hair,
yellow bright even in the gray, clouded afternoon. He
could see a long-skirted brown dress but not much
else as the woman leaned from one side of the wagon.
She seemed to be studying the ground as she drove.

The big man's eyes lifted to peer a few hundred
yards ahead of where he rode. The four half-naked,
bronzed forms were still there, paralleling the wagon
below on their sturdy, short-legged ponies. They had
watched the lone wagon for almost two hours, just as
he had. The big man's lips edged a tight smile. He
knew exactly what they were thinking. It was almost
built into the Indian attitude, regardless of the tribe.
He brought his gaze back to the wagon below, a big
Owensboro mountain wagon fitted with top bows and

a canvas top. No Conestoga but serviceable enough for a long, hard trip.

A bitter sound came from his lips. Alone out here, she might have a hard trip, but it wouldn't be a long one. Maybe she had a good reason. The big man frowned, though he couldn't think of one that didn't add up to monumental stupidity. A long breath escaped him, drawn from deep down in his powerful chest. He wanted to ride away. He couldn't go risking his neck to play Good Samaritan for every damn fool in the West. But he wouldn't ride away, he swore softly. Logic and reason were no match for conscience.

He'd go down to her. He'd give her a chance to survive, at least another day. His eyes went to the four horsemen who moved with ghostlike silence through the mountain ash. They'd see him when he moved down to her, of course, but there was no other way. Maybe it would be enough to make them move on. Maybe . . .

He pulled his lips back in a grimace as he turned the Ovaro up onto a higher ridge of thick tree cover. He put the horse into a trot and passed the four Indians on the ridge below. He continued on for another few hundred yards before he sent the Ovaro downward. The tree cover was heavy and he was far enough ahead. The four braves wouldn't see him until he emerged in the open down on the flat land.

Riding straight down, brushing against the smooth gray-brown bark of the ash as the wooded ridge grew more dense, the Trailsman emerged onto the flat land at the bottom just as he saw the wagon come over a slight rise. He moved toward it and reined up directly in her path and saw her bring the wagon to a halt some twenty-five yards from him. He slowly walked the Ovaro forward. She was young, he saw, and at close range the yellow hair was flaxen, loose, and shoulder-length. He took in a strong but very attractive face, classical in its lines, well-defined cheekbones, a straight, thin nose. Eyebrows only a shade darker than the flaxen of her hair were thin arches over robin's-egg-blue eyes. Her lips were a little thin, perhaps because of the way she was holding them. The brown dress rested against a slender figure with a nice swell of breasts under the square neckline.

He saw her hand move to the seat beside her and come up with a long-barreled .54-caliber army rifle. "That's close enough, mister," she said, and Fargo halted. The rifle barrel was rock-steady, he saw, and he smiled.

"You'll not be needing that for me," he said.

"It stays," she said evenly.

"Taking no chances. Very smart."

"Thank you," she returned coolly.

"Except it makes me wonder."

"Wonder what?"

"What the hell you're doing out here all by yourself like a goddamn fool."

Her robin's-egg-blue eyes flared. "That's my business," she snapped. "What do you want, mister?"

"Name's Fargo. Skye Fargo," the big man said calmly. "You've got yourself some company."

"I can see that," she sniffed.

"Not just me, honey. Four braves up on the ridge line. They've been riding along with you for the past two hours," Fargo said. Her eyes shot up to the thick tree cover on the ridges, scanned the scene for a long minute before turning back to him. "You won't see them. Not until they want you to," he said.

"But they're up there?"

"That's right," he said.

"For the past two hours?"

"Just about."

"That means you've been riding along all that time, too."

"Right again," he said.

He saw her eyes studying him for a moment. "Then, why haven't they come after me?" she questioned, more condescension than concern in her tone.

"Indians are real careful. One thing they hate above all else is being ambushed. It hits at their prowess as warriors," Fargo said. "But they're not only careful, they're logical."

"Meaning what exactly?" She frowned.

"They can't believe anybody would be so goddamn stupid as to come out here all by themselves," he said, and saw blue sparks in her eyes. "So they've been waiting and watching to make sure you're not the bait to sucker them into a trap. Soon as they're convinced you're not, they'll pounce on you quicker than a red-tail hawk on a gopher."

The young woman's eyes moved up to sweep the thick trees on the ridge lines again, narrowed as they searched for any sign of movement. Finally they returned to the big man in front of her. "And you've come to help me," she said.

"That's the general idea," he said, and saw the skepticism in her eyes as she stared back. "You don't believe me, do you?"

"My mother told me always be careful of strangers who want to do you favors," she said.

"Sometimes a mother's advice is good. Sometimes it's not worth shit. This is one of those times," Fargo said, and felt himself growing impatient.

"Why don't you ride along ahead of me, about where you are, for the next few miles?" she said. "If they attack, you'll be here to help."

His smile was made of ice. "I'll be a sitting duck, the first one they'll take out. No, thanks, honey."

"You want to be in the wagon with me," she said.

"Or next to it," he replied.

"Sorry, I'll have to pass on that," she said firmly, and he realized he couldn't blame her. She was alone, wary, and not about to swallow a stranger's story about being watched by Indians. It was simply the wrong time for her rightful skepticism, and the rifle barrel's unwavering steadiness told him he'd not be convincing her any further. Her words echoed his thoughts. "Now, I'll be moving on, and I suggest you go your way, Mr. Fargo," she said. "And I thank you for your concern."

"Good manners and good looks. Very nice," Fargo said.

"You forget about the goddamn fool part?" she tossed back.

"No. That still goes," he said cheerfully, and paused to watch her blue eyes flash before turning the Ovaro away. He felt her eyes watching him as he moved into the trees, to disappear from her sight. He paused, glanced back, and saw her roll on.

He rode upward toward the ridges. She wasn't the only one who had watched him leave, he knew, and he climbed the steep hillside to the first ridge and moved east through the trees. He rode with relaxed casualness, but all his wild-creature senses were tuned to the trees at his back. It took only a few minutes for him to pick up the horse and rider following through the mountain ash.

They were being completely predictable. They were probably Chippewa, he reckoned. He had expected they'd send one of their band to see where he went.

Fargo kept the Ovaro at a walk eastward along the ridge. The Indian hung back and would have been invisible to most men. The other three would do nothing till he returned, Fargo knew, and he had gone perhaps half a mile when he became aware that he was alone. His follower had left, convinced he was nothing more than a passing rider. Fargo swung the Ovaro in a wide circle and headed back the way he had come, taking care to stay back far enough not to be seen, heard, or smelled.

He kept glancing downward through the trees, but the wagon was still not in sight. It wasn't for another quarter-mile that he saw the four bronzed riders below, moving downward from the ridge. He glimpsed the wagon ahead, then, and saw one of the Indians spur his pony forward, still in the trees but almost at the bottom of the hillside. Fargo slowed and saw the other three move on until they were abreast of the wagon. It was then that he caught sight of the fourth Indian as the man emerged from the trees a dozen yards in front of the wagon.

The other three braves were suddenly moving fast, heading for the flat ground almost abreast of the wagon. Fargo spurred the Ovaro forward. He saw the young woman bring the rifle up as the one Indian blocked her path. He watched her draw a bead on the Indian, rifle to her shoulder, waiting. It was only when the Indian suddenly sent his pony charging forward that she fired. But the brave was ready for the rifle shot and flattened himself across the pony's neck. The shot went harmlessly over his back.

The young woman tried to get off another shot when two arrows grazed her shoulders from the right side of the wagon. She half-turned, ducked as another two shafts slammed through the canvas of the wagon. She tried to bring the rifle up to fire again, but the Indian had reached her from the front. With lithe grace he dived from his pony and sent her flying backward on the seat. The rifle fired into the air and he tore it from her grasp.

The other three braves had halted alongside the wagon and one started to climb from his pony onto the driver's seat of the big Owensboro.

Fargo reached the edge of the trees and pulled the big Sharps from its saddle case. The rifle was at his shoulder as he skidded the Ovaro to a halt. He fired and one of the Indians on the wagon did a backward somersault as he flew from the driver's seat in a shower of red. The two still on their ponies alongside the wagon whirled and one flew backward from his pony as if on invisible wires. He hit the canvas side of the wagon and left a wide smear of red as he slid lifelessly to the ground.

But Fargo had no time to get off a third shot as he saw an arrow hurtling straight at him. He had to duck, flatten himself across the Ovaro's neck as the shaft grazed his back. He looked up to see the Indian charging directly at him, his pony galloping full out.

Fargo tried to bring the big Sharps up for another shot, realized he had time only to swing the stock of the rifle upward to parry a vicious swing of a tomahawk. The blade of the short-handled ax hit the rifle with such force that Fargo felt himself fall sideways from his horse. He hit the ground on his back, shot a quick glance across at the wagon, and saw the fourth Indian pulling the girl onto his pony.

"Damn," he spit out as he felt the hoofbeats thundering toward him. He rolled and saw the tomahawk slide along the side of his temple as the Indian delivered a swooping blow. He rolled, ended up on his back to see that the brave had already spun his pony around.

Fargo managed to pull the Colt from its holster as the red man charged at him again. On his back, he fired from the hip as the charging horse bore down on him. He saw the rider suddenly quiver and a red hole explode in the center of his chest. The man toppled forward with a guttural cry, landed facedown on the ground, and lay still. Fargo pushed backward, flung a glance at the wagon, and saw the fourth brave disappear into the trees on his pony, his arms wrapped around the young woman.

Fargo swung to his feet and ran to the Ovaro. A long upward dive put him in the saddle and the powerful horse was in full gallop in seconds.

He didn't slow as he raced into the trees, confident of the Ovaro's ability to maneuver and keep its speed. He gained ground quickly and saw the flaxen hair through the trees, a bouncing yellow beacon. He could hear the heavy snorted breathing of the Indian pony as it slowed, its short-legged barrel-chested body too chunky to skirt the dense trees. Fargo glimpsed the Indian make a sharp swerve to the right and disappear into a heavy cluster of box elder.

The Trailsman followed, the Ovaro deftly slipping

between two tree trunks. Fargo plunged into the box
elder and suddenly yanked the horse to a halt. He could
hear the Indian pony, but the animal was drawing in
deep breaths of air. He'd stopped and Fargo cursed as
he dived from the saddle as two arrows slammed into
the tree trunk barely inches away from him.

He hit the ground on his side, winced at the impact,
but rolled and came up with the Colt in his hand, fired
two shots into the trees, and dropped to one knee.
He caught the movement of brush to his right and the
Colt was aimed at the spot as the Indian emerged, the
young woman held in front of him, a hunting knife
against her throat. He halted and pressed the edge of
the knife blade to her skin until a trickle of red
appeared. He barked a command and Fargo didn't need
to understand the language to get the message. He hesitated a moment and saw the terror in the girl's eyes;
with a silent curse, he tossed the Colt onto the ground.

The Indian flung the young woman away instantly
and charged forward, the hunting knife held out-
stretched. Fargo's eyes stayed on the blade as he
counted off seconds, let the charging figure come a
few steps closer, and as the point of the knife seemed
about to plunge into his chest, he dropped almost to
his knees. The Indian bowled into him and Fargo rose,
slammed one shoulder into the man's abdomen, and
the square, stocky form staggered backward with a
grunt of pain. Fargo swung a long, looping left that
caught the man alongside his jaw, and the Indian staggered backward.

Fargo sprang forward to deliver a hard right, cursed
at himself as he realized he'd been too hasty. The
hunting knife was coming at him in an upward arc,
and he managed to twist his head to one side and felt
the blade whistle past the tip of his jaw. He flung
himself sideways and a slashing sweep of the knife just
missed ripping into his shoulder. He hit the ground
facedown, rolled, and came up on one knee to see his
foe coming at him with quick, agile foot movements.

The Indian feinted and Fargo reacted, twisted away from another blow of the knife, and let himself seem to stumble backward, off-balance. With a roar of triumph, his opponent leapt forward, the hunting knife upraised. But the big man suddenly stopped stumbling backward. Instead, he dropped low as the knife slashed empty air over his head. He brought up a piledriver uppercut that crashed into the red man's jaw. The Indian staggered backward, trying to shake sudden cobwebs from his head. Fargo's left arm shot out, his hand closing around the Indian's wrist. He twisted and the hunting knife fell from the man's fingers.

Fargo flung the man aside and dived for the knife on the ground. He had just closed his fingers around the hilt when he felt the figure diving at him from behind. There was no time to turn or look around, and he lashed out in a backhanded blow with the knife. He felt it connect and heard the gargled sound as the Indian fell half atop him. He sprang to his left and felt the man's body slide away, and he whirled to see the Indian futilely pawing at his throat with one hand as his lifeblood poured out.

The man fell to both knees, still making strangled sounds, and finally pitched onto his face. He quivered for another moment and then lay still.

Fargo threw the knife into the underbrush and turned to see the young woman on one knee. She pushed to her feet as he reached her, breasts straining the neckline of the dress as she drew in deep gulps of air. The fear began to leave her eyes as he led her to the Ovaro and swung into the saddle behind her.

It wasn't until they returned to the wagon that she spoke. "Is it over?" she asked.

"I think so, but I'm not going to take any chances," Fargo said as he peered down at the still forms on the ground. He grunted. "Chippewa. I figured as much. They're not real bad, but they're not real friendly, either. Let's get out of here."

"I've something to say," she answered.

"Later," he said. "Take the reins." He watched as she stepped into the wagon with a graceful movement, and he motioned to an opening in the trees.

"I was going north," she said.

"Not now. Others might come looking for these. We take cover. Besides, you've less than an hour of daylight left," he said, and moved forward to lead the way into the woods. He found openings barely wide enough for the big Owensboro, but he watched with satisfaction as the fresh forest grass quickly sprang back to obliterate tracks. The forest grew thicker and the dusk quickly turned it into a place of shadowy shapes that made further travel dangerous.

When the front corner of the wagon splintered against a tree he called a halt. "This'll do. We're in far enough," he said. "No fire."

He dismounted, unsaddled the Ovaro, and leaned back against a tree trunk in the dimness. He felt the dampness of the night seep through the forest. An edge of wind reminded him that he had seen the last of the downy foxglove and oxeye daisies a few days ago. The bright red of the cardinal flower and the purple-fringed orchid, too. It would be up to the deep pink of the morning glory and the black-eyed Susan to bring color to the land now. He saw the shadowy form swing from the wagon and come toward him, the flaxen hair pale silver in the last of the dark dusk.

"You saved my life, Fargo. I can't ever repay that. But I owe you a very big apology, and I can do something about that," she said.

"I'll settle for an explanation," Fargo answered. "I want to know what in hell you're doing out in this country all by yourself?"

She settled against the tree trunk next to him and he smelled the faint muskiness of her, a mixture of powder and perspiration, somehow strangely attractive. "It wasn't supposed to be this way," she began.